P9-APA-864

BACK
OF BEYOND

by Dvora Waysman

PITSPOPANY

NEW YORK ◆ JERUSALEM

Back of Beyond: A Bar Mitzvah Journey
Text copyright © 1996 Dvora Waysman
Cover Art: Chana Navon

ISBN: 0-943706-54-8

Published by PITSPOPANY PRESS
All rights reserved

Printed in Channel Islands

EYTAN M. GOLDSCHEIN

DEDICATION

To my Australian family,
Bobbie (Roberta) Rhine
and Philip Opas Q.C.

EYTAN M GOLDSCHEIN

FROM THE AUTHOR

There are many people who helped me along the way to "Back of Beyond." I would like to thank my publisher, Yaacov Peterseil, for his creative input; artist Chana Navon and designer Benjie Herskowitz for the imaginative cover; and Dr. Amram Miller and cultural attache David Stark at the Australian Embassy for valuable reference material. Lastly, but most importantly, my editor Chaim Mayerson — it was a joy to work with him!

I have provided a glossary of Australian words, commonly called "BUSH TALK," on page 139 of this book.

BACK
OF BEYOND

CHAPTER ONE

Danny's eyes grew wider and wider as he continued reading:

"In the Dreamtime, when animals were people, Karra-Karra the Cuckoo-Woman traveled with her husband along the beach on a dark, stormy night. They had many young children with them, and they were looking for a place to hide from the rain..."

He was reading his favorite magazine, *Habitat*. He'd gotten a subscription as a gift from his parents on his twelfth birthday. Every issue focused on a different country, and this one was the most exciting one he'd received. It was all about Australia and the native people called Aborigines who lived in the very center of this enormous land.

He'd already read how these dark-skinned people, who were described as Stone Age hunters, gathered food. There was plenty of fish, berries, roots and grubs, as well as kangaroos, to hunt.

Australia, Danny learned, was not only a country but a full-fledged continent. It was an enormous island the size of the United States without Hawaii and Alaska. For centuries, the Aborigines had Australia to themselves. But from the sixteenth century onward, explorers from Europe searched for the continent they were sure existed. The first one to land there was a Dutchman, Captain Willem Jansz, who came in 1606, but when he didn't find any gold or silver he left. The next was Abel Tasman, who came to the continent in 1642 but also couldn't find the riches he was after.

A century later, a British traveller, William Dampier, landed on the West Coast, but he also left empty-handed, describing the Aborigines as "the miserablest people in the world."

It was Captain James Cook, the great British navigator, who saw the land for what it really was. He landed in 1770 from his ship, *The Endeavor*, and claimed all the territory for King George III, the king of England.

"Danny, have you done your homework?" Danny's mother asked.

"Almost," he said, looking up from the magazine.

Mrs. Goodman came into his room. "What does that mean?"

"I'm reading."

"Work for school?"

"I'm reading *Habitat*. It's very educational."

"So is your homework," she reminded him. "Danny, you promised me that first —"

"I know. Okay, I'll finish the algebra first," he said, his eyes losing their sparkle.

I wish I didn't have to go to school, he thought. If only I could just study the things that interest me. I wish I could be someone who goes to exciting places, and maybe even live with natives — or an explorer, or one of those archaeologists who dig for jars and statues and coins and things from the past. Algebra! Who needs it? Nevertheless, he reluctantly put the magazine aside and took out his math book.

But as soon as he finished, he got back to the story about the Cuckoo-Woman. The Aboriginal legend told how Cut-Cut, the Spirit Man, went into the air and rolled many waves of dark over the country, waves like clouds, which kept it dark for endless days. Karra-Karra's husband had gotten lost, and Cut-Cut offered to find him if she would just give him one of her children. Every few days Cut-Cut would come back to say he hadn't been successful, but he

Dvora Waysman

would look further if she gave him another one of her children.

Finally, when he had taken her last child, Karra-Karra knew that her husband would never return, and she was terrified that the Spirit Man might take her, too. She ran into the bush, and, among the trees, she changed herself into a cuckoo bird. From then on, she never made a nest, because she was afraid that if she tried to raise little ones, Cut-Cut would return to take them away. And that is why to this day the cuckoo lays its eggs in the nests of other birds.

"Wow!" Danny said aloud. He loved these stories. He looked at the pictures of the Australian Aborigines, illustrating the legends that were both their beliefs and their folklore. The grizzled, muscular, dark-skinned Aborigines had learned to survive in the inhospitable, fiercely hot interior of the continent by moving on all the time, like nomads, looking for food and water.

Danny closely examined the pictures of their animals — no domestic ones, only the ferocious, dog-like dingoes. He remembered a story that had grabbed international headlines a few years earlier when a woman at Ayer's Rock in Northern Territory claimed that a dingo had stolen her baby and eaten it. The dingo looked like a cross between a dog and a wolf, and Danny decided he wouldn't like to come in contact with those sharp teeth.

The article went on to describe how the different legends took place in the Dreamtime, what the Aborigines called *Alchera* (all-cheer-uh). The Alchera was a time when their ancestral spirits walked the earth. The Aborigines taught their children that the spirits that sleep beneath the ground rose and traveled about then, shaping the landscape, forming people and teaching them the art of survival. When the spirits finished their work, they went back to sleep. Today, the article said, the Aborigines in central Australia still reenact these myths. They go on ceremonial wanderings that they call "going walkabout," where they dig water holes, build rock shelters, hunt kangaroos and perform secret rites.

Danny felt he was entering a secret world when he read *Habitat*. His friends, who enjoyed science fiction, computer games, comics and videos, thought he was a bit crazy. But Danny felt that real-life people and places were much more fascinating than games and fiction.

As he was flipping through the other articles in the magazine, he came across a page marked, "Enter the Back of Beyond Contest." Australia was launching a new national airline and wanted suggestions for an interesting and unusual name. First prize was a round trip for two, all expenses paid, to Australia. The winner could spend three weeks visiting any part of the vast continent he or she chose.

For the next few days, Danny was obsessed with the contest. He tossed restlessly in bed at night, but no name good enough to win came to mind.

He asked his sister Rebecca to help him. After all, she was sixteen and seemed to know everything, or so she said. "Koala Airlines," she suggested. "You know, those cuddly little bears that live in eucalyptus trees."

He frowned. "Only about fifty million people will think of that. Can't you be more creative?"

His best friend, Joe, didn't do much better. "What about Boomerang Airlines? Yeah, that's a good name. The airline that takes you round trip. Get it? But if you win, remember it was my idea and I'm coming with you."

When Danny didn't react, Joe explained, "Don't you know what a boomerang is? You throw it at animals, and when it knocks them senseless, it comes back to you."

Danny couldn't resist pulling his friend's leg. "Sure, but think about this. When someone gives you a new boomerang, how do you ever throw the old one away?"

Joe actually scratched his head trying to figure out the problem, but when Danny laughed, Joe realized it was a joke.

Unruffled, Joe asked again, "So what do you think?"

"About what?"

"Boomerang Airlines?"

Danny tried to be kind. "It's not original enough. It has

to be a name no one else will think of. Don't forget, this isn't a contest just for kids. It's for grown-ups, too. But I'm going to win it!"

Danny reread the article, playing with different words. The writer described the interior of the continent where the Aborigines lived as the *"Back of Beyond"* or the *"Never-Never."*

"I couldn't call it Never-Never Airlines," Danny mused. "People might think they'd never arrive or were on their way to visit Peter Pan. And back of beyond sounds like a trip into space."

For the umpteenth time he studied the article. These nomadic people survived in the blistering-hot interior of Australia, hunting and gathering wild fruits and roots. They also ate things like witchety grubs, the larva of a species of longicorn beetles, which the Aborigines found very succulent. Ugh! Danny shuddered to think about it. Centuries ago, they'd also been cannibals, and occasionally women would eat their babies, because, as the article said, "they were very fond of baby meat." But the essence of the Aborigines lay in their myths and legends, the Dreamtime they called Alchera.

"That's it!" Danny suddenly shouted out loud. "They're the original Australians. It should be a word in their language. They thought their ancestors flew over the earth, and this airline will be flying around the world. What better name for an Australian Airline than the Aboriginal word for Dreamtime — Alchera Airlines!"

Danny mailed his entry to the airlines a few days before the deadline. He didn't just send in the name. He had always wanted to write a commercial, so attached to his entry was a whole advertising campaign he had designed around the word "Alchera."

When Rebecca asked him what name he'd sent in, he just smiled. "Okay, so don't tell me," Rebecca snapped. "I'll bet it's something stupid anyway, limp-brain."

Joe was also upset when Danny refused to reveal the name. "So what's the big secret? You probably sent in a blank entry anyway."

It was hard for Danny to concentrate on his studies for the next few weeks while he waited for the November issue of *Habitat* to arrive, announcing the contest winner. He was frequently scolded by his teachers at Maimonides Day School for daydreaming. Rabbi Goldberg, who was teaching him the portion of the Bible, called the *Torah* in Hebrew, he would have to chant for his *Bar Mitzvah*, was especially annoyed. "You'd better get your act together or...," he warned, giving Danny the distinct feeling that he was going to make a fool of himself when he got up to read in the synagogue.

A few days before the November issue was due to arrive, Danny came home from school to find his family sitting in the living room with a stranger. They were drinking lemonade and looked excited, happy and a bit worried all at the same time.

"Danny," his mother said quietly, "Mr. Williams has something to tell you." Mr. Williams stood up and extended his hand. He was a big, suntanned man, and his handshake almost crushed Danny's fingers.

"Congratulations, Danny," he said warmly. "I'm from Alchera Airlines. You have won our contest. Yours was by far the most original entry."

Everything happened at once. Rebecca actually hugged him. His father boomed "*mazel tov*" several times, thumping him on the back and smiling broadly. His mother was crying her "I'm proud of you" cry.

"You don't look very surprised," remarked Mr. Williams.

"Oh, I didn't think anyone else would come up with a better name," Danny said. "I just hoped you'd realize how good it was!"

"How conceited can you be?" Rebecca yelled, but everyone else just laughed.

After all the excitement died down, his father, looking very serious, said, "Danny, we have a problem."

Danny waited. Nothing was going to spoil this trip for him. Nothing.

"You see, Danny, the prize was meant for two adults, like a husband and wife. Not a twelve-year-old boy."

"So you or Mom can come with me," he quickly responded.

"It's a bad time for me, Danny," his father told him. "I've just started up my own business. I'm sorry, son, but it's too soon for me to go away for three weeks."

A lump formed in Danny's throat. "Mom?"

"How can I leave Ruthie for three weeks? She's still a baby. She's not even walking yet. And I have to make the arrangements for your Bar Mitzvah. Invitations, seating and everything. And I hate to say this, but according to Rabbi Goldberg, you're not nearly as ready as you should be, Danny. This may not be the time for you to go."

"That's a good point," his father added. "How will you finish studying for your Bar Mitzvah?"

"It's still five months away," he pleaded. "I'll be ready. I'll study hard even while I'm away. It's only for three weeks."

Suddenly, Rebecca said quietly, "I could go with him."

Danny looked at her in surprise. Usually she pretended he didn't even exist.

"How old are you?" asked Mr. Williams.

She drew herself up tall. "I'm sixteen."

John Williams shook his head. "I'm sorry. If you were eighteen..."

Danny turned to face the window so they wouldn't see that his eyes had filled with tears. Mr. Williams looked at the mop of curly brown hair under the skullcap. The shoulders that had been so straight only a few minutes ago were slumped. If Danny had looked at Rebecca, again he would have been surprised to see that the look of disappointment in her eyes mirrored his own. She really felt sorry for him.

After a short silence, Mr. Williams said, "I guess we could provide an adult escort for Danny and Rebecca. Would you agree to that, Mr. and Mrs. Goodman?"

"Well, I suppose..." his mother said, looking at her husband, who nodded his approval.

There was a rush of words, but Danny heard only music, like ten orchestras playing a great concerto. The words drifted over his head: "...someone reliable...kosher food... enough rest...access to a doctor if they got sick...insurance..." All he knew was, it was really going to happen.

Although his older sister wasn't usually his favorite companion, Danny appreciated how she'd offered to join him. They would fly to Australia, the biggest island in the world, and he'd have an adventure he'd be talking about for the rest of his life!

What Danny didn't know was that the three weeks in Australia would almost be "the rest of his life"!

CHAPTER TWO

The next two weeks passed like a dream for Danny. It was decided that he and Rebecca would leave in late November, the beginning of summer in Australia, so that they could be back home in time to celebrate Hanukkah with the family. Their parents convinced Mr. Williams to be their escort — his practical common-sense manner had impressed them — and Alchera Airlines agreed.

The portion of the Bible Danny would read in the synagogue for his Bar Mitzvah was called *Tzav*, the Hebrew word for command, from the Book of Leviticus. Danny had to learn to read it in perfect Hebrew and chant it according to special musical notes called *ta'amim* or *trop*. His teacher recorded the tune for him, which Danny promised to listen to regularly.

There had been a few arguments with Rebecca before they left.

"I won this trip, and I'm not wasting it on silly things we can do at home," Danny informed his older sister when he learned about her planned shopping forays. "You go shopping all the time in New York, Rebecca. I want to see unusual people and places that I'll always remember and do exciting, different things. I've got it all planned out. You'll enjoy it, too. I'm sure you will."

"So where do you want to go?" Rebecca asked, sulking.

"Just listen to my idea. You'll love it!"

"Says who? Okay, I'm listening."

"We're going to Ayer's Rock."

"A disco?" Rebecca asked, hardly believing her ears. "A *yeshivah* boy spending his time in a disco? And you think my ideas are dumb."

"Don't be ridiculous. It's a real rock — an enormous red monolith."

"You've been reading too many of those weird magazines. You win three weeks in Australia, and we're going to spend it visiting a rock! Well, if you think I'm going to agree to that, you've got rocks in your head!"

"You don't understand," Danny said insistently. "Ayer's Rock is incredible. Let me show you the picture. Look, it says it's 1,150 feet high and five miles long."

"I don't care if it's as big as Mount Everest. I'm not going there — and don't forget, baby brother, if I don't go, you don't go, either!"

"Oh, yeah? Mr. Williams is going to be the escort, so I can take anyone I want.. I can take Joe."

"Even Joe won't spend three weeks on a rock," countered Rebecca.

"At least he'd let me tell him about it."

"What's to tell? What could possibly be interesting there?"

"If you keep quiet for five minutes, I'll tell you. This Ayer's Rock is in the part of Australia they call Northern Territory. But it's not called Ayer's Rock anymore. They use the Aboriginal name of *Uluru*."

"It doesn't matter what they call it. It's still a rock, and I don't want to go there! And how did Aborigines get into this conversation?"

"That's what's exciting. They're the original Australians that lived there for centuries before the white men arrived."

"Okay, so now added to the exquisite fascination of a rock, we have a population of natives, who probably can't talk English. I can hardly wait!"

"You're a racist, Rebecca. You know that?"

"I am not. I just can't imagine what we'd have in common. I think you're crazy. What are we going to do there for three weeks?"

"Well, it'll be fascinating to explore. Anthropologists spend years studying other peoples and cultures under primitive conditions. We're going to have the chance to do it in comfort, and maybe see things no Americans can even imagine. This Uluru is supposed to be holy to the Aborigines."

Danny's eyes were shining, but Rebecca's were filled with tears.

"You're really selfish," she blurted out. "You just don't care that I'll hate it."

Before he could answer, the phone rang. Rebecca answered and fought to control her voice.

"Oh, hello, Mr. Williams. Yes, he's here. No, to be honest, I'm not excited. I'm depressed. Danny wants to spend the entire time on some dumb rock.... What's it called? Yes, that's it, Uluru. I mean to say... We could go to Coober Pedy on the way? I've never heard of it. They mine opals there? Wow! I just love opals. Do you think... Cheap? Really? I'd be able to get some jewelry. Promise? And we could stay there for a few days?" Rebecca hung up the phone. Danny was amazed to see his sister dance across the room.

"Danny, my contest-winning brother, a valuable opal necklace will soon adorn this feminine throat. Can't you just see it? Milky white, flashing with iridescent colors... What did he say the mining town was called?"

"Coober Pedy," her brother answered in disgust. "Didn't Mr. Williams want to speak to me?"

"Oops, now that you mention it. Sorry, I guess I got carried away."

"So you've changed your mind about coming?"

"It's called compromise, brother of mine. You get your rock, but I get my stone!"

Mr. and Mrs. Goodman became very nervous as the big day approached. After all, they were sending their two older children off to the other side of the world, to a different hemisphere. Danny's father tried half-heartedly to persuade him to postpone the trip for six months so he'd be able to go with him. His mother called Mr. Williams daily with more questions and requests — so many that Danny got really embarrassed.

Finally, the big day arrived, and they left for the airport. The jumbo jet was waiting for them at Kennedy Airport, and so was Mr. Williams. "Look, Danny," he said, pointing, "you made it happen." In enormous gold letters, all along the length of the plane, gleamed the words:

"Alchera Airlines.
For your Dreamtime flight."

It was Danny's prize-winning slogan.

"Soon you'll be seeing commercials on TV and hearing them on the radio. We're using some of your ideas, Danny," he said, slapping him on the shoulder.

Danny couldn't do anything but grin as he and Rebecca followed Mr. Williams onto the aircraft that would carry him to his great Australian adventure.

It was a ten-thousand-mile journey to Australia, and although both children had flown on domestic flights, this was the first time Rebecca and Danny had been outside the United States. Even Rebecca, who tried to act blasé, as was appropriate for an older sister, couldn't conceal her excitement at the prospect of the eleven-hour flight to Adelaide. From there they would begin their inland trek to Coober Pedy and Ayer's Rock.

They enjoyed the flight immensely. They learned about Australia from Mr. Williams, who insisted that they call him John. One of the in-flight movies was *Crocodile Dundee* which gave them their first taste of what would be waiting for them in the Australian wilderness, or — as the Aussies called it — the *Outback*. Danny was happy to see that Rebecca seemed to be getting more enthusiastic by the minute.

John Williams also seemed to be a great escort. He was a third-generation Aussie, whose great-grandparents hailed from England. He managed to dispel some of the stereotypical images they had picked up from the movie.

"Do you think we'll see crocodiles?" Rebecca asked with a shiver.

"I think it most unlikely," John answered. "Sure, *Down*

Under, as Australia is popularly called, is an extremely interesting land, but you really don't meet absurd, lovable animals wherever you go. In fact, seventy percent of the population live in the ten biggest cities. Few people have ever seen a koala dozing in a eucalyptus tree or a kangaroo suckling her joey — a baby kangaroo — except in a zoo."

"Are all Australians so strong and athletic?" Danny asked. He couldn't help but notice that John seemed to resemble the star of the movie in height and stature.

John laughed. "I guess most of us are fanatics for the outdoor life. But we certainly don't all live in the Outback, rounding up cattle and swilling beer. I spend most of my working day behind a desk."

The next morning, they landed in Adelaide. The modern international airport was as comfortable and efficient as any back home. It was a bright, sunny day, and John arranged a tour of the city, with its parks and gardens, elegant squares and broad boulevards. Rebecca was delighted when they visited the art museum, and while Danny was no fan of museums, he was thrilled to examine the world's largest collection of Aboriginal artifacts.

"It's a beautiful city — really modern," Rebecca commented with some surprise. John laughed.

"Once, not so many years ago, this was a really sleepy town, and people from Melbourne and Sydney used to joke, 'I went to Adelaide once, but it was closed!' But now, like any big city, it has its museums and nightlife, as well as its seamier side."

After an exhausting day of sightseeing, they spent the night at a luxurious hotel. Danny, who shared a room with John, kept his promise and practiced his Bar Mitzvah portion. John, who'd never heard Hebrew before, was fascinated.

"What does it mean?" he asked.

"Well, the part I'm practicing now is about blood. It explains why Jews can't eat just any kind of meat."

He found the English translation for John:

> *And you shall eat no manner of blood, whether it be of fowl or of beast, in any of your dwellings. Whosoever it be that eats any blood, that soul shall be cut off from his people.*

"Pretty scary stuff, eh?" John commented. "Why can't you eat a nice, rare steak, for instance?"

"Well, the truth is that we can. We're not allowed to eat blood by itself, and we have to do whatever we can to get as much blood as possible out of the meat before we eat it. We have a special way of soaking and salting it to do that. It's called *kashering*. Even so, you can't get every last drop of blood out, so once we've kashered the meat, we can grill it and eat it even a bit rare. My rabbi once suggested we have to get rid of the blood to tame our instincts for violence — sort of to give us a horror of bloodshed."

"That makes sense," John agreed.

It was a new experience for Danny to have to explain his religion and its customs to someone not Jewish, but he felt comfortable talking to John, who seemed genuinely interested. Danny and Rebecca were also very appreciative of the fact that John never ordered non-kosher meals to the room. They shared their vacuum-packed kosher meals with him.

"I'll eat what you eat," he said with a laugh. "Maybe my violent instincts could do with some taming, too!"

CHAPTER THREE

They travelled the six hundred miles northwest from Adelaide to Coober Pedy in an air-conditioned bus. Until they actually stepped off the bus, neither Danny nor Rebecca realized just how hot it was. "Sizzling" was the only word Danny could think of to describe it. The temperature was 113° Fahrenheit, and John told them that in a few more weeks, as summer got into stride, it would probably rise to a "somewhat uncomfortable" 122 degrees.

"How do people live here?" Rebecca asked, perspiration pouring down her face. "And where is everyone?"

"That's a surprise," John answered. He took them to a door in the side of a low hill. It led to a vast underground city. Inside, the temperature was quite comfortable. It seemed like a city out of some sci-fi film.

"There are about two thousand people living here," he told them. Danny's eyes widened. Some of the homes they passed were quite luxurious. They passed a bank and a church before they reached their air-conditioned motel.

"We'll be here for just another day," John told them. "Very early in the morning, before it gets too hot, we'll go out and look at the opal fields. I've even got a permit for you from the Mines Department to go noodling in the mullock heaps."

"To do what, where?" asked Rebecca.

John laughed. "You have to get used to talking Strine — that's our Australian slang — while you're here. 'Noodling' means fossicking."

"I think I liked noodling better," Danny grinned.

"And what does fossicking mean?" his sister added.

"I keep forgetting you're American. I suppose you'd call it sifting. The mullock heaps are the rubble at the top of each mine shaft. I've got rakes and sieves for you. You sift through the rubble, and, if you're lucky, you might find an overlooked opal."

"Oh, wouldn't that be wonderful," Rebecca exclaimed, delighted at the prospect of finding a real jewel. Danny laughed at his sister's enthusiasm as he recalled the bitter arguments they'd had in New York about the itinerary for the trip.

"It's not easy in this heat, and truthfully you probably won't find any opals," John continued. "But even if you don't, I'll take you in the afternoon to a demonstration of opal cutting and polishing. You can also buy opals there and have them set into a ring, necklace, bracelet or earrings. They're much cheaper here than in the city. In fact, I think you'll be surprised how little they cost at Coober Pedy."

The underground motel was very attractive, and the rooms were just as comfortable as those in the hotel in Adelaide. The receptionist, Irene, took a liking to the youngsters from America and invited them to visit her that evening for a cup of the favorite Australian beverage — tea.

Irene lived in a *dugout* close by, and Rebecca was amazed that her apartment was so similar to those in New York. The underground temperature was quite cool, and Irene's kitchen had most of the same appliances as their mother's kitchen. Irene wore a large opal ring that Rebecca kept admiring.

"Did you find the opal here?" she asked.

Irene shook her head. "No, this is a boulder opal. You don't find them here. Coober Pedy's opals are white, milky stones. This comes from the Outback, in Queensland. My husband found it embedded in a rock there. When we get tired of Coober Pedy, we'll move to Lightning Ridge in New South Wales. My husband's a miner, and he wants to try his luck with the black opals they have there."

"Are they really black?" Danny asked.

"Well, I guess they're more blue than black. But they are the rarest and most expensive of all. That's where Bob thinks we'll make our fortune."

"Mining must be a hard life," John commented.

Irene shrugged. "You could say that — feast or famine, really. I work at the motel for our bread and butter during the in-between times."

While they were talking, her husband, who'd been reading a bedtime story to their little boy, came in to join them.

"What is an opal exactly?" Danny asked.

Bob, a big, strong Aussie like John, smiled at him. "Forgive the pun, but about opals, I'm a mine of information." He laughed at his own joke, then became serious. "Well, they're quartz-like stones. You find them embedded in the most ordinary rocks, just waiting to be found. Coober Pedy is Australia's biggest opal field. In fact, most of the world's opals are produced here. Opals are actually hydrous silica, a jumble of submicroscopic crystals. They're only mined for their beauty. You can't use them for industrial purposes like you can diamonds. I've seen them in every color imaginable: white, yellow, green, blue, red and black. They make marvelous jewelry, even if they're not all that valuable."

Bob excused himself for a minute and returned carrying a rake and sieve. He handed them to Rebecca. "You'll be needing these tomorrow. This set once brought me luck. I found a black opal the size of an egg with it."

"More like a grape," his wife teased.

At first Rebecca refused the gift, but when John said it was an honor to get these utensils from a miner, she accepted.

They drank tea and talked about America, which made both Rebecca and Danny a bit homesick.

"We'd better get back," John announced. "We have to be up at dawn to do our mining."

"Noodling," Danny interrupted. "Although I think I'd rather fossick," he added, starting everyone laughing.

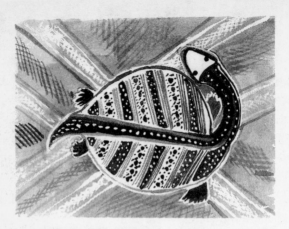

CHAPTER FOUR

While normally a late sleeper, the next morning Rebecca was up, banging on Danny and John's door, at dawn. Impatient for the day to begin, she was already clutching her rake and sieve. It was another half-hour before they were ready. Danny had to say his morning prayers, and then they all had breakfast before setting out for the minefields. Even so early, the sky was red with the promise of another searingly hot day.

Rebecca was fascinated as she churned through the mound of rubble, convinced that the next stone would contain a brilliant, flashing opal. Danny's heart wasn't really in it. The stones were monotonously uniform, and sweat was soaking his armpits and running down his back. He soon gave up and moved to the shade of a shelter erected nearby. An old prospector was squatting there. He must be at least eighty years old, Danny thought. The grizzled old man was unshaven, his teeth yellow and misshapen, and his skin looked like tough, old leather.

"How ya goin' mate?" he greeted Danny.

"How do you do?" Danny replied politely.

The old man chuckled. "Mighty formal, aren'tcha. My name's Barney," he volunteered, extending what looked like a grubby paw.

Hesitantly, Danny shook the old-timer's hand. "Uh, my name's Danny."

"Oh, you're a Yank. We get lots of 'em here — tourists like. Gonna make your fortune?" Barney chuckled again.

"I doubt it. We haven't found anything yet, and, anyway, opals are not very valuable, are they?"

Barney screwed up his eyes against the sun. "Don't be too sure, lad." He tapped a dirty finger on his cheek. "I been here for years. I was here in '56 when they found the big 'un."

"How big was that?" Danny asked, feigning curiosity.

Barney grinned. "It weighed seven and a half pounds — can you believe that? The bloke what found it was set for life — sold it for $1.7 million. Never worked another day in his life."

"Have you ever found a big one?" Danny asked, just to

keep the conversation going. The shabby, old prospector hardly looked like a success story, but you never know.

"I've 'ad my moments, 'ad my moments," he repeated mysteriously. "Not lately, but there's always today or to-morrer.... How long ya here?"

Danny found it very hard to understand his accent. He seemed to swallow either the first or last syllable of every sentence. "We're going up north tomorrow to Ayer's Rock. We're spending a week there."

"Ain't called that no more. They call it by its Abo name now — Uluru. I can talk some of the Abo jabber y'know." He was silent for a minute. "Know what Coober Pedy means?" Danny shook his head. "Means 'white man's hole in the ground.' Pretty clever fellas, the Abos."

"Do they speak English?" Danny asked.

"Sure, most of 'em. Kids go to those mission schools and so on. But they got their own lingo, too. Used to have doz-ens of languages. Now there are about twenty that they still use. Government here's changing all the place names back to their lingo — to make 'em feel proud, ya see."

"What other names have they changed besides Ayer's Rock?"

"The Olgas — call 'em *Kata Tjuta* today."

At Danny's blank look, Barney laughed. "Don't know the Olgas? Just west of Uluru ya'll find 'em. Real big moun-tains with thirty-six domes. Abos say they were once just

one big mountain, much bigger than Ayer's Rock even."
Barney was thoughtful. "Had an Abo mate once — good
bloke. He was one of them *Anangu*. That's the tribe that
lives there. He taught me some of their lingo. Want to hear
it?" Danny nodded politely.

"*Pukulpa Pitjama Ananguku Ngurakuta.*"

"What does it mean?"

"Welcome to Aboriginal land." Barney paused to light
an ancient and evil-smelling pipe. "You'll be arriving in the
wet, won't ya?"

When Danny's expression went blank again, the prospector laughed. "Only have two seasons in the Back of
Beyond where you're goin' — the wet and the dry. Wet be-
gins in November. Lasts till April. Might get cyclones,
hurricanes, typhoons. Funny weather in the Never-Never.
Better look out for *Water Hole Jalliung,* too."

"What's that?"

"Abos say it's a bottomless pool and home of a magic
snake what devours any strange fella who drinks from it."

In spite of the heat, Danny shivered. "It's just another
one of those legends to scare children, right?"

Barney was thoughtful. "Can't be sure. Once, when I
was with my mate, I thought I heard the voice of *Nalja*. It
scared us, ya can be sure."

"Who is Nalja?"

"He's the spirit of an old, old man with white hair. His

voice comes from the hair beneath his armpits. If you look at him, you die!"

Danny was stunned for a moment. The old man was describing exactly what he had read about in the Torah. There had once been witches that spoke from their armpits. He remembered their name, *Ovot* (Vayikra 19:31). The Torah warned the Jews not to take on the practices of these witches when they entered the Land of Israel. This was a revolting form of idol worship. But no one said that their black magic wasn't real.

"Do you really believe all that stuff?" Danny asked, feeling goose pimples on his arms.

"Mebbe I do, mebbe I don't. Abo fellas got a lot of magic we don't understand. Boys your age got to know their past before they start what they call 'initiation' to become a man, you know."

Danny was excited. "Really. That's interesting because I'm Jewish, and in my religion, when a boy turns thirteen, he also becomes a man. We are also supposed to know our past, our Torah, before we enter manhood. And we have a ceremony, too."

"What kind of ceremony?"

"It takes place in our synagogue, where we pray," Danny explained. "We call it a Bar Mitzvah — 'a son of the commandment.' There are 613 commandments all told, plus lots of do's and don'ts that help keep you within the fold, so to speak. My Bar Mitzvah is in four and half months. I have to learn special prayers, and I'll read from the Bible in Hebrew."

"That's all? One day?" the old man asked.

"Well, the ceremony part is short but —"

Barney snorted. "That ain't nothing. Them Abo boys got to pass nine tests. Takes a few years. Have to show how brave they are. Each test worse than the one before. Lotsa blood," he added, shaking his head.

Before Danny could ask what he meant, a yell came from Rebecca, who was still fossicking. John was congratulating her while she jumped up and down with excitement. In her hand she held a stone in which was embedded a beautiful milky white opal, a rainbow of iridescent colors radiating from it.

CHAPTER FIVE

Danny and Rebecca would never forget their first sight of Ayer's Rock — Uluru. The world's largest rock, it protruded from a buried mountain range. John Williams had told them that it was 1,150 feet high and five miles wide, but no words could have prepared them for the actual sight. It stood alone in an endless, flat landscape. The rock was tinted a rich copper red, which made it seem as though it were on fire. You couldn't imagine that it would be possible to scale it. The almost perpendicular ridges revealed that at one time the horizontal beds of stone had been tilted upwards.

They were flying in soon after dawn to minimize exposure to the searing heat. As the first light of day touched

Uluru, the rock seemed to be about to explode. It glowed red and orange as it emitted what Danny was sure were rays of wondrous power.

Every now and then, Danny would reread and quote from *Habitat*.

"You know, Northern Territory covers one-sixth of the whole area of Australia, and Australia itself is as big as forty-eight mainland U.S. states, or twenty-four times as big as the British Isles."

"Oh, give it a rest," Rebecca groaned. "That's the third time you've read that part to us. I don't think you practice your Bar Mitzvah reading that much!"

Catching a glimpse of Danny's downcast face, John came to his rescue. "Actually, Rebecca, it's very interesting. Most people don't understand that Northern Territory alone is the size of France, Spain and Italy combined. You can drive for hours to reach the next town on the map, and when you get there, you discover it only consists of a petrol station, a general store and a pub. In fact, some of the remote farms we are flying over are so big that cowboys round up their cattle by helicopter. There's one ranch that's actually the same size as Belgium."

Rebecca had the grace to be ashamed of her rudeness and was nice to Danny for the rest of the flight. By the time they landed, she and Danny were friends again.

Ayer's Rock had its own airport and a hotel complex to

accommodate the thousands of foreign tourists who visited each year.

"What do you think?" John asked them proudly, the sweep of his arms encompassing the modern, attractive hotel right in the middle of the never-never country.

"Fantastic," said Rebecca, whose fingers kept touching her opal pendant. She had been allowed to keep the stone she had found, and it was her greatest treasure, especially since it had been made into a beautiful pendant. She was looking forward to having time to really study it. Irene, back at Coober Pedy, had persuaded her not to go for a traditional setting. Instead, the opal had been cut from the stone in a solid hunk, the back of which was dipped in silver. It was now almost a triangular shape, broad at the base and narrowing at the top, from where it was suspended on a thin, silver chain. The opal itself was milky white, and when it caught the light, veins of color radiated from it in purple, deep blue, rose, green and lilac. Rebecca thought it was the most beautiful necklace in the world, and even Danny, who thought jewelry was a waste of money, admitted it was "interesting."

"Danny, you're very quiet," John commented.

"I didn't expect to find a hotel. I thought we'd sleep in a tent or at most a trailer. It just seems too civilized."

John laughed. "Maybe it is out of place in such an isolated spot, but many tourists wouldn't come to the Red

Center, as they call this part of the interior, without it."

"I'm certainly not going to say no to air conditioning," Rebecca asserted. "The heat and humidity are unbearable."

"You're just spoiled, Rebecca. You don't know what 'pioneering spirit' means," Danny said, more to impress John than to scold her.

Rebecca was about to answer with a biting reply, but a frown from John stopped her in her tracks. After all, she realized, if it hadn't been for Danny winning the trip, she certainly would never have had a chance to fly to Australia, and her opal pendant wouldn't even be a dream. Rather than fight, she resolved to find a way to show her gratitude.

Later, after they'd finished unpacking, they sat in the hotel lounge sipping cold drinks. Danny noticed a boy around his own age sitting by himself, staring moodily out of the tall, wide windows that encircled the lobby. Danny ambled over to him.

"Hello," he said, sitting down uninvited.

The boy nodded.

"I'm Danny Goodman," he volunteered.

"Grant Evans," the boy grunted, not showing much interest.

Feeling a bit foolish, Danny nevertheless continued. "I'm from New York. Are you from overseas, too?"

"Naw, Aussie. Born in Sydney. Miss it, too. Been here eleven months. My Dad's the manager of the hotel." Grant spat out his entire spiel like someone who had been through it all dozens of times before.

Undaunted by the boy's robot-like response, Danny said, "Must be exciting to live here."

That brought a rise from Grant. "You gotta be kidding! Just that big red rock. Nothing to do. You can go off your head." Then, with a look of longing on his face, he asked, "Been to Sydney?"

Danny shook his head. "We were in Adelaide. That was pretty neat."

Grant snorted. "Adelaide ain't nothing. Sydney — that's a city. Fantastic surf beaches. Full of life. Only things that move here are the flies," he said, disgusted.

"You'd love New York," Danny offered. "It's an enormous city, loaded with people and things to do."

"So why'd you want to come here?"

"I won a prize for naming the new Australian Airline 'Alchera.' Know what it means?"

"Sure I do. Alchera's the Dreamtime."

Danny was both surprised and impressed. "How do you know that?"

"I live among the Abos, don't I? Haven't got any real white friends here."

"Would you introduce me to some Aborigines?" Danny asked excitedly.

Grant shrugged. "If you like. Muri works here. Want

to meet him?"

"Now?"

"Why not?" Grant said, getting up.

The two boys were just about to leave when John called, "Hey, Danny boy, where're you off to?"

"Going to look around the hotel with Grant," Danny answered, introducing his newfound friend.

"Don't forget your homework," John reminded him. "I promised your mum."

"Later," Danny promised. "We won't be long."

"Thought you were on holiday," Grant commented as they walked out of the hotel.

"Yeah, but I'm missing school, and it's near the end of the year. Where's your school?"

"Don't go. I learn by correspondence."

"That must be great," said Danny, who always felt confined by the school curriculum. He longed to study only the things that interested him.

Grant shrugged. "A bit lonely. My mum supervises my work, and she's tougher than ten teachers. 'Course, I could go to the mission school where Muri used to go, but it's Roman Catholic and we're not."

Grant led them to the olympic-sized swimming pool near a beautiful garden. The man-made, tiled pool disturbed Danny. It was totally out of place in the Back of Beyond, the Never-Never. He wanted desperately to recapture the feeling of awe they'd experienced at their first sight of the enormous red rock rising so majestically from the earth. He would have preferred a waterfall emptying into a cool pool of water. Not some chlorinated, lukewarm swimming pool.

The garden around the pool also bothered Danny. It looked like a deliberate attempt to civilize the wildflowers and native plants that grew in great profusion on their own. Giant gum trees, the Australian name for eucalyptus trees, provided welcome shade. They filled the air with the fragrance of eucalyptus whenever a breeze ruffled them. But they had been planted in neat rows, rather than left to grow willy-nilly as in the wild. There were different varieties of flowering acacia and plants Danny recognized from the pictures in the *Habitat* article, like desert pea and kangaroo paw. All seemed picture perfect. Almost as though the plants have been tamed, thought Danny.

Working in the garden was a boy around their age.

"Muri, this is Danny," Grant said as he walked over to the Aborigine. "Want to come for a walk with us?"

When Muri saw Grant, he put down the spade. A set of flashing white teeth split his dark face. Although he was slim, with thin black legs protruding from his shabby khaki shorts, his arms were strong — bulging biceps already straining the fabric of his short-sleeve shirt. His denim shirt was open to the waist, and the buttons had clearly fallen off. His big brown eyes held a mischievous twinkle that lit up his whole face, and a mop of curly black hair flowed down the side of his face, reminding Danny of the sidelocks he had seen on *Hassidic* Jews who sometimes came to pray at his synagogue. Most striking, however, was his nose, which was pierced with what appeared to be a small bone.

Muri tapped his wrist where a watch would be if he owned one. "No walk now. Not time yet. Break much later."

"It's nearly time. I'll ask my Dad if you can stop for a while and come with us."

Grant revealed a sudden spurt of energy as he dashed back inside the hotel.

Muri and Danny sized each other up.

"I'm twelve — almost thirteen," announced Danny. "How old are you?"

Muri held up first his ten fingers, then another three, smiling shyly.

"Do you speak English?" Danny asked, and then felt foolish as he'd heard him speak to Grant.

"Pretty good at white fella's lingo," Muri asserted.

"Do you live with your family?"

Muri shook his head. "Not with women now."

"Not with your mother?"

Muri drew himself up tall. "Me *nimma-nimma* now. Live with all single men in front of married men's huts.

Soon be a man myself."

Grant came hurrying back. "It's okay, Muri. Dad says you've done enough for this morning. Come back to work on Thursday morning. You can walk a bit with us now."

Muri nodded and went to put away his spade.

"What does 'nimma-nimma' mean?" Danny asked Grant.

"Sort of initiation. He has to pass nine tests before his tribe thinks he's a man. He's only passed two so far. It takes a few years. They get harder and harder."

Danny remembered his conversation with Barney, the old prospector at Coober Pedy. "Which two has he passed?" he asked curiously.

"Had to be circumcised. That was the first one. Know what that is?"

"Sure," Danny said hastily. "In my religion, all baby boys have to be circumcised when they're eight days old."

Like Barney, who had thought Bar Mitzvah ceremonies were nothing much, Grant was unimpressed. "Ain't nothing when you're a baby. Muri was eleven."

Danny felt a chill run through his body. "And the second?" he asked hesitantly, not sure if he wanted to know.

Grant pointed. "See what's in his nose?"

"Some kind of bone?"

"Yeah. They have a kind of feast — a dinner, with the men of the tribe sitting round him. Then the *yagoo* — that's the person who's gonna help him become a man — puts a small bone from a kangaroo paw through his nose. Then they eat all the food. Next day they take out the first bone and put in a turkey bone. Hurts like mad!" Grant said cheerfully.

"How do you know all about it?"

"He's my mate, ain't he? We hang around together when he comes to work at the hotel. Tells me lots of stuff."

Just then Muri rejoined them. They left the hotel grounds and walked toward the giant monolith, Uluru. Dusk was falling, the shadows lengthening, and the dying rays of the sun caught the huge stone, setting it ablaze just as Danny had first seen it that morning.

"Wow!" he said, lost for words.

"*Kuniya* made it," said Muri, following Danny's gaze.

"Is that your word for God?" asked Danny.

Muri shrugged. "Kuniya big fella carpet snake. When it was Alchera, in Dreamtime, Kuniya camped and hunted by water hole on a big sandhill. Sandhill turn to stone. Now it's Uluru."

Danny knew from his reading that Aborigines used their legends to explain the creation of pools, hills, jumbled stones, lakes, rivers and rocks. Still, standing there looking at Ayer's Rock silhouetted against the sky, he thought of a giant carpet snake called Kuniya and started to wonder.

CHAPTER SIX

The next morning, John had arranged to accompany Danny and Rebecca on a climb up Uluru. A bus took them, their guide and a few other tourists the twelve miles to the base of Ayer's Rock. It was so huge, Uluru had seemed only yards away when they looked through their hotel window.

"Which climb are you ready for?" John asked them on the bus, reading a brochure he'd picked up at the hotel. "You can choose: The Climb, which it says in this leaflet is a mile and takes two hours round trip to reach the top and return to the base; The Liru Walk, which is one and a quarter miles, but it is less steep and takes only thirty minutes each way; or The Uluru Circuit Walk, which is six miles and takes four exhausting hours to complete."

"Let's take that one," said Danny enthusiastically. "We've got all day."

John looked dubious. "The heat's a killer, Danny. I doubt if Rebecca could do it. I'm not sure if I could," he said with a laugh.

"I stood up to Coober Pedy," she reminded them. "I was still out fossicking or whatever you call it, while Danny was sitting under the shelter."

"That's true," Danny admitted, glad to have his sister on his side. "Does that mean you're ready to try the big one?"

"Well, actually — no." Danny's face dropped. "Let's take the medium one — what did you call it?" she asked John, trying to work out some sort of compromise.

"The Climb," he said, noticing Danny's forlorn expression. "Trust me, Danny, you'll thank me once you feel what the baking temperature is like."

Then, taking out another leaflet entitled *Surviving the Never-Never*, John said, "I don't want you to come down with heatstroke or anything, so lets go over some of the precautions they advise. I know we talked about them at the hotel, but it never hurts to recap.

"You must wear a hat to protect you from the sun. Also, I stuck a couple of umbrellas in our bag, which may seem ridiculous, but at this time of the year it can suddenly start pouring. I was a Boy Scout once, and our motto was, 'Be prepared.' Most important of all, we must keep together. I've got the map, so no going off on your own," he cautioned Danny.

"You're prepared for anything," Danny commented, brightening a bit. "What else have you got in that backpack?"

"Food — lots of it. Climbing's heavy work."

"What kind of food?" Rebecca asked.

"Well, there's dried fruit, fresh fruit and hard-boiled eggs, and, of course, big bottles of water. Danny, you can take the first-aid kit and one of the water bottles. Rebecca, you carry another canteen of water and the insect repellant. I don't want the flies and ants to have us for lunch. I've got a compass, whistle, bandages and some rope, just in case." John divided up the load.

Danny laughed. "In case of what? It can't be such a big deal. It's just a climb up a big rock."

"A lot of things have happened to people in Northern Territory because they thought the environment was no big deal! The rule for most Aussies who work the Outback is, if you think you don't need it, you will! I'm responsible for you kids, so I'm not taking any chances."

When they got to Ayer's Rock, they looked up. The view of the wall of stone going straight up to the sky was scary. The group of tourists seemed like ants looking up at an elephant's foot. It was still early, but the intensity of the heat had already sapped some of the tourists' energy, and they started swigging from the water bottles even before the climb had begun.

Rebecca didn't see much point in climbing the rock and would have been happy to stay at the ranger station, which had a display of Aboriginal arts and crafts at the souvenir kiosk. But she didn't want her brother to call her a coward. Worse still, without her, he might decide to take the more dangerous route, and she didn't want to be responsible for what might happen.

Before they began, a ranger warned the group that the climb should not be attempted by anyone with a medical condition. Immediately two middle-aged people dropped out, so there were only eight people climbing — John, Rebecca, Danny, four other tourists and their guide, Bill.

Danny learned that, even with the help of a safety chain, the climb *was* a big deal. After they'd been climbing for about forty minutes, they were dripping with sweat. The guide called a rest period. Danny, tired but by no means exhausted, saw a hollowed-out formation in the rock, like a small cave.

"If you still have the strength to explore some, go ahead," the guide told Danny. "I think you'll be impressed by what you find in there. We'll rest for another twenty minutes."

Danny persuaded Rebecca and John to go with him.

The hole was just big enough for Danny and Rebecca to climb inside, while John waited outside the cave for them.

Inside, they could just barely stand straight. There were lights set up throughout the cave. On one of the walls was an Aboriginal rock painting that looked as if it had been there for centuries.

"What is it?" Rebecca whispered.

Danny peered closely at the painting. It was carved into the rock and painted in white, brown and yellow clay with some red ocher and charcoal. It looked like a snake, a crab and a possum surrounded by dots and curves.

"I think the snake is Kuniya. Muri told me that he created Uluru," Danny whispered back. "I don't know about the possum."

"Why are we whispering?" Rebecca asked.

They both began to giggle. "It's kind of creepy," Danny admitted.

They crawled out again and told their guide what they'd seen.

"You're right about Kuniya the Carpet Snake," Bill told him. "The others are Rureru the Crab and Parray the Possum."

"Who are they?" Danny asked.

"According to the legend, Parray the Possum lived near Rureru, who was a very old blackfellow, as they used to call the Aborigines. Rureru had never learned to play the *didg-*

eridoo (did-jury-do) like Parray. The didgeridoo is one of the Aborigines' musical instruments, made out of a hollowed branch. Parray and Rureru were friends, and while Parray played, Rureru would dance. Every night Parray would play for him. But one day Parray became tired of this and suggested they go their separate ways because he wanted everyone to hear his music. Rureru begged him to play that night for him for the last time. He danced harder and faster, moving backwards towards the beach. He called out to Parray that he couldn't hear the music anymore, so Parray climbed a hollow tree and began to blow on it, and the sound was even stronger than the crashing waves. Rureru danced backwards into the sea but was too tired to care. 'I'll stay here and become a crab,' he told himself. And that's why crabs, to this very day, move backwards."

John clapped Bill on the back. "Did you just make that up? It's a good story."

"No, not at all," said the guide. "I know many of the Aboriginal legends. They're all part of the *Dreaming*, the web of beliefs that binds their people together in life and after death."

"The Dreamtime?" asked Danny, thinking of his Alchera Airlines.

"No! They mean different things. The Dreamtime is their time of creation; the Dreaming is their belief and value system."

Suddenly, a strange wailing sound pierced the air.

"Listen, what's that noise?" whispered Rebecca.

Again it came, louder this time. The wailing sound seemed to be coming from everywhere at once.

The whole group stood rooted to the spot. Then John pointed high above them. Silhouetted on top of Uluru, against a reddened sky, an Aborigine was playing on a hollowed tree branch that was about five feet long. It was a didgeridoo, like the one they'd just heard about from Bill. The man's body seemed to be moving in rhythm to the ageless wail of the didgeridoo. As they watched, hypnotized by the music and his swaying, another figure joined the first, and there was the accompaniment of the *clapping sticks*.

Mournful music filled the air. It seemed to be a message, a type of code that described the strange happenings of the Dreamtime, when men and animals had changed their forms to become the ancestors of all that inhabited the earth. It was eerie listening to these ancient tunes, and the music somehow sapped the climbers of their desire to continue.

By unspoken consent, the small group began descending Ayer's Rock. They did not speak above a whisper to each other as the music followed them like a shadow to the base of the giant monolith.

Danny was deep in thought as they boarded the bus back to the hotel. He couldn't shake the notes from his head. He felt they were more than just sounds of the past, more than the songs of ancient Aboriginal heroes and gods.

Somehow he sensed in this music something sinister and dangerous — as though the two men at the top of the rock were trying to send him a warning.

CHAPTER SEVEN

The next morning, the strange feelings that had overcome Danny at Uluru had passed, and he was ready to explore again and hear more of the legends.

John Williams had slipped coming down the rock. At first he had thought nothing of it, but by morning his ankle was swollen. The doctor advised him to rest it for a day.

Rebecca still hadn't woken up. Chances were good she would sleep until noon, so Danny banged on her door until, sleepy-eyed, she came out. She wouldn't hear of going back up the mountain but readily agreed to spend some time shopping with her brother.

The souvenir store in the lobby held a vast array of bird, fish and reptile totems, or emblems, of different Aboriginal tribes. The birds and fish were carved from wood, and the reptiles were made from fiber, feathers and paper bark, carefully painted and decorated. Rebecca wanted to buy one, but Danny was against it.

"They're idols, Rebecca. I don't think Jews are allowed to have them."

"Don't be silly," she said peevishly. "I'm not going to worship them. They're just pieces of unusual art."

"Just the same, they are holy to the Aborigines. I don't think you should buy them."

"Okay," Rebecca said crossly. "So what do you suggest I buy, a Barbie doll?"

Danny chose to ignore her remark. "Those bark paintings are pretty neat," he said. "I bet they would give you something to talk about with your friends."

They examined the smooth inside sheets of bark that had been stripped from trees. The Aboriginal artists combined all kinds of natural materials to make spectacular patterns with clumps of dried spinifex grass molded into circles and curved lines.

"Won't they fall apart?" Rebecca asked the saleslady, an Aborigine who wore a badge that said, "My name is Nyanngauera."

"No, ma'am. We learn to bind edges. They don't curl up."

Danny and Rebecca each bought a small bark painting

for themselves and some boomerangs as gifts for their parents and friends. Nyanngauera carefully wrapped each item. As she was putting the boomerangs into tissue paper, she remarked casually, "These created from our ancestor god Bobbi-bobbi's ribs. You see shape? He made boomerangs to help our people hunt food so they survive."

Rebecca's eyes were wide. "In my religion, we believe that Eve, the first woman, was created from the rib of Adam, the first man."

Nyanngauera nodded. "I hear that story at the mission school. Good story!" she commented.

"You don't believe it?" Danny asked.

She shrugged. "I hear many stories from the Bible when I go to mission school. Boomerang look like rib, not woman. I believe legends from my people, from my mother and my grandmother Kabbarli. They tell me about Altjira, sky god with feet like emu, and about Kulu, the Moon Man. They stories in my blood." She waved to a figure passing the window. Danny saw that it was Muri with his shovel and hose.

"You know Muri?" he asked.

"He my brother," she said as she finished wrapping the last of their purchases.

Rebecca took the gifts to her room, while Danny raced outside, despite the sizzling heat, to find Muri. The Aborigine was slowly digging around some shrubs, pulling out weeds, while Grant sat in a canvas chair watching him. Muri flashed a wide smile at Danny as he joined them.

"Take the load off your feet," Grant said, motioning to a vacant chair near the pool. Danny felt uncomfortable to be sitting while Muri was working, but eventually he pulled a chair over to Grant.

"Maybe we should help Muri?" Danny suggested.

Grant laughed. "Does he look like he's overworking?"

"Well, not exactly," Danny said, smiling.

Muri heard him and joined the laughter. "Too hot work hard," he said.

"It's always too hot for you to work," Grant teased.

Muri laughed again and strolled off to attach the hose to a tap at the end of the garden. Grant confided that his father gave Muri work mainly because he was Grant's friend and needed the income.

"He tidies up a bit, that's all. And if he doesn't turn up occasionally, Dad still pays him. His sister works for us, too."

"Yes, I met her in the gift shop — Nyanngauera."

Grant looked surprised. "Yeah, that's her. We call her Nyan for short. How old do you think she is?"

Danny hazarded a guess. "Twenty-five?"

"She's only fifteen, but she's married. She got married last year. Her husband's the yagoo that's going to help Muri become a man. Remember I told you?"

"The one that put a bone through his nose?"

"Yeah, she hasn't got any babies yet, so she works for us. She really works hard. Not like my mate Muri." Grant laughed. "Well, I'm off for a swim." He got up abruptly and performed a showy dive into the pool.

When Muri returned, Danny told him, "I met your sister inside."

Muri nodded. "Boss like her. He pay her lotta money. She manage shop," he added proudly.

"Grant says she's married. She's very young."

Muri shook his head. "No, she old. She fifteen. Our girls marry twelve, thirteen..."

Danny laughed. "Then my sister Rebecca's an old lady already. She's sixteen."

But Muri was serious. "Yeah. White women marry very old."

"When will you marry?" Danny asked him curiously.

"When I a man. Few more years. Have to be a member of clan first."

"Is that like a tribe? In my religion, there were twelve tribes, but ten of them are lost."

"We no get lost," Muri said simply. "Many clans, many totems. Always find our way."

"What's your clan?"

"I an *Aranda*," Muri said proudly. "Lizard is our tribal ancestor, our totem. Why you not swim?"

"I like talking to you. I learn things. It's okay, isn't it? I don't want to get you into trouble with Mr. Evans."

"Tomorra I no work. Tomorra I walk. You come with me?" he offered.

"That'd be great. Where will we go?"

Muri shrugged. "We just walk. Nice places."

"I'd really like that," Danny said excitedly, "but I'll have to ask John first."

"Who John? Your father?"

"No, he's our escort." Seeing that Muri didn't understand, Danny tried to explain. "Our parents are in America. They couldn't come with us. We're on a trip, a kind of holiday," he added, not wanting to boast about his prize. "John's looking after us."

By Muri's blank expression, Danny realized that he hadn't heard of America and couldn't fathom why an "old woman" of sixteen like Rebecca would need looking after, so he gave up.

"If I can come, where can I meet you?"

"Outside hotel. Sun up?"

"That's too early," said Danny, thinking that first he had to recite his morning prayers and have breakfast. He knew Muri didn't have a watch.

"Two hours after sun up?"

Muri shrugged. "I wait awhile. You not come, I go alone."

"What about Grant?"

"He gotta do schoolwork with Missus Evans. He tell me."

"I'll go ask John. I'll come out anyway to tell you. You wait."

Muri flashed another wide smile. "Be nice if you come," he commented. "Lonely sometimes."

Danny found that persuading John to let him go was not easy.

"I'm not keen about it Danny. I'm responsible for you."

"But I can't stay cooped up in the hotel all the time."

"I realize that. You won't have to once my ankle is better. How do I know where you'll go and how long you'll be? You're not used to this heat. What if you get lost?"

"I'll take water. I can't get lost with Muri. Grant says he knows every inch of this territory. I want to explore, and what a great opportunity to do it with an Aborigine. Wow! What a terrific story I'll have when I get back to New York."

John was very reluctant to give his permission. He had a premonition that it wasn't a good idea, but the excited look on Danny's face won him over.

"Okay, mate," he said in a resigned tone. "But I want you home before dark, mind. And try to stay out of the sun. I don't want you coming down with heatstroke."

Danny was elated. He raced outside to tell Muri the good news. As he was running to the pool, he ran straight into a giant, frilled lizard sunbathing on the path. The lizard opened its mouth, and around it, a swath of skin unfurled like an umbrella. It stood on its hind legs, rocking menacingly from side to side, and emitted a scary hiss before disappearing into the garden.

It was a full minute before Danny calmed down enough to look for Muri, but the Aborigine was nowhere to be found.

"I hope he'll be here tomorrow," Danny said to himself. Then he remembered Muri telling him he was from the Aranda tribe.

"And the Aranda tribe totem is a lizard," he said ominously.

CHAPTER EIGHT

Danny didn't know how long Muri had been waiting for him the next morning, but the young Aborigine showed no sign of impatience.

"You come!" he said simply and happily. "We walk!"

They set out at a brisk pace. Danny hoped that he'd be able to keep up in the heat. He was wearing a straw hat, but Muri was bareheaded.

"By the way, where are we going?" Danny asked.

Muri pointed vaguely to the northwest.

"Is that on the way to that big thirty-six-dome mountain range? The Olgas? I've forgotten what you call them."

"Kata Tjuta."

"Right. Well, they're a long way, but I suppose we could

at least try. Will we be back for lunch?"

"Plenty food."

Danny looked at Muri's empty hands. "I brought some sandwiches and drinks. But by late afternoon we'll be hungry again."

"Plenty food," Muri repeated.

Danny assumed they would visit friends of Muri's on the way. They had already passed a few huts with children playing outside, and some of them had waved to Muri.

The landscape was spectacular. They were walking over the relics of an immense bed of sedimentary rock. Windblown sand stung Danny's legs. Occasionally, despite the desert terrain, there was a pool of water where frogs croaked, and twice Danny saw a snake slithering under the rocks. It made Danny think of Kuniya, the giant carpet snake. There were hundreds of plant species that Danny had never seen before.

Whenever he asked a question — and in the beginning they came pouring out — Muri would just smile and grunt. Danny wasn't sure if Muri understood him, or if he just preferred not to talk. He could see that Muri was happy just to plod on in companionable silence, and for Danny, too, it was oddly comforting after awhile just to listen to the sounds of nature all around them.

Most of the time the land was flat, but every once in awhile they had to slither over steep slopes. Slippery algae and lichen formed multicolored patterns. It was unlike any landscape Danny had ever seen. It wasn't the kind of desert you would imagine, with occasional cacti growing. Because of the Northern Territory's long, wet season, between red sandhills grew stately desert oak trees. Danny was grateful for the occasional shade, as the heat was blistering.

"Can we rest for awhile?" Danny asked, swigging from the water bottle and really beginning to suffer from the intense heat.

"No hurry," Muri assured him. "We rest long time. No have to be at work or school," he joked. He seemed to have endless patience for the weaknesses of his white friend, and when Danny sat down, Muri sprawled out beside him.

Once Danny stumbled over a rock and disturbed a large, frilled lizard like the one he'd encountered the day before. Although it was small, it began to hiss and lash out with its tail.

"Don't be fright," said Muri. "Only Tannar. In Dreamtime," he went on to explain, "Lizard Man Tannar got caught in big storm. He wanted to go into Wonbri's cave. Wonbri Black Snake Man. But Wonbri mean. He tell him he not move seashell from door, and Tannar have to drill it. He did. Plenty hard work. But when he pushed his head through the hole, Wonbri had spear.

"'You go 'way,' he tell Tannar, 'or I kill you!' But Tannar no can pull head out of the hole in the shell. Now he the shell on his neck forever. That extra skin you see on lizard. But Tannar got even," Muri said with satisfaction.

"What did he do?" asked Danny.

"After storm, Wonbri climbed a big hollow tree in the bush. Tannar followed him. When Wonbri tried to climb down, he fell on Tannar's shell and cut legs off on sharp edge. Wonbri say, 'I have no more legs. Now must be black snake and crawl on belly.' Tannar, he become frill lizard. He like to frighten people, but he okay. Not poison."

"I think we should start going back to the hotel," Danny announced. He didn't want to admit that he was starting to worry. They had eaten all the food, and his feet were sore. He was sure they had covered at least fifteen miles.

"Not yet. Good to walk," responded Muri.

"Well, sure. But don't forget we have to walk back, too." Muri was silent.

Danny was becoming uncomfortable. They had long passed any huts or signs of human life. At one point, they had climbed a kind of fence made from tree branches. When Danny asked what it was, Muri ignored the question, and Danny had let it pass.

"Muri, I want to start going back," Danny persisted.

"Now we on sacred tribal land. You can't go back."

"What?" Danny almost screamed.

"Black men kill you. Not let you go back now." Muri said matter-of-factly. "You be my brother. Live here with me," he offered.

"No! I have to get back!" Danny shouted. A wave of panic overpowered Danny.

"You no find the way," Muri said, a little smile of triumph at the corner of his mouth.

Danny looked back across torrid tablelands and patches of dense rain forests. It was true. They had not followed any track discernible to Danny's eyes.

"You tricked me," Danny yelled accusingly. "Take me back. Rebecca and John will be frantic."

"Few days," Muri agreed. "Now I go walkabout — not want to be alone."

"We have no food." Danny tried to suppress the panic in his voice.

"Berries, roots, ants, grubs — plenty food."

"But I don't eat those things..."

"You hungry, you eat," Muri assured him.

The long red shadows began to lengthen. Although it was still hot, Danny found himself shivering.

"You become my brother. Maybe you want to stay here."

"No, you don't understand. I have two sisters...."

Muri smiled. "Sisters different. Brother something else!"

"And I have parents across the ocean."

"You almost man now. No need parents."

"But I do." Danny choked back a sob.

"I look after you," Muri assured him kindly. "I teach

you things you never learn in school. You can be brave hunter."

Danny sensed it was useless to argue. He had to find a way to persuade Muri. Tomorrow. He was tired...so tired. He sank down near some spinifex, in the shade of an acacia tree, and was soon fast asleep.

CHAPTER NINE

It was the middle of the night when Danny felt Muri gently shaking his shoulder. He sat up abruptly, at first not knowing where he was. Then it came back to him. He was somewhere back of beyond, far from civilization, lost between Uluru and the Olgas mountain range. He could be anywhere on the ninety-mile stretch that separated the two giant sites sacred to the Aborigines.

"I make you dinner," Muri said softly. "You hungry." Danny opened his eyes wide. A fire blazed inside a ring of stones, and he remembered that, as he'd fallen asleep, Muri had been rubbing two sticks together. He drew close to the fire that crackled as it threw out small sparks. Despite the searing heat of the day, the night was cold, with a dismal wind blowing the sand in their faces. He'd gone to sleep in the open, but while he'd slept, Muri had evidently built a kind of shelter for him out of branches and grass.

"*Gunyah*," Muri explained, gesturing toward his handiwork. "Keep you warm till morning."

Although some hours earlier keeping warm had been the furthest thing from Danny's thoughts, he realized that now he was grateful — both for the gunyah shelter and the fire that crackled and sent out a comforting heat.

On a nearby rock, Muri had set out "dinner." Danny couldn't recognize anything, but he knew, hungry as he was, that the laws of keeping kosher made it necessary to question everything carefully. He pointed to a pile of food that smelled very tempting.

Muri seemed to admire his culinary choice. "Witchety grubs. Very good." Muri speared one with a twig.

"Er, no...no thanks," Danny said, recoiling in horror.

"You taste. Very good. Like nuts," Muri insisted, passing the twig with the blackened bug to Danny.

"No, I can't. I'm a vegetarian," Danny blurted out, hoping Muri had heard about vegetarianism.

Apparently he had. "I got vegetable foods, too. These yams," Muri informed him, holding out another stick with an orange yam.

"How did you cook them?" Danny asked suspiciously.

"Dig out of ground. Put on fire."

"You didn't rub anything on them first?"

"Nothing. Fire burns off dirt. I no lie to you!" Muri exclaimed, for the first time showing emotion. Danny wanted to tell him that he had lied in leading him out into this wilderness, but this wasn't the time to argue. If Muri got really angry, there was no telling what he might do.

"Mmm, tastes good," Danny agreed, biting into the sweet potato. It did taste wonderful, better than anything he had ever eaten at home. He looked at his watch. It was two A.M. No wonder the yams tasted so good. It was thirteen hours since he'd eaten!

"Here berries. No meat. You bite. Very good. Juice. Like water. You no be thirsty."

Danny took some of the little red berries between his fingers. They looked like the red currants his mother sometimes used to make jam.

"You're sure they're not poisonous?"

Muri laughed. "I not dead. I eat every day."

Reassured, Danny bit into them. They were tart and very refreshing. He swallowed the juice gratefully, while Muri contentedly munched the pile of fat grubs.

Once he had taken the edge off his hunger, Danny decided to try and reason with his Aboriginal friend.

"Muri, I appreciate what you're doing. Looking after me and all that."

"You my friend. Maybe soon my brother," Muri answered, his cheeks filled with grubs.

Danny tried not to think of the bugs Muri was crunching like peanuts. "No, that's what I want to explain. I can't be your brother. I'm too different from you."

"You white. I black. But not so different."

"You're right about that part, but it's just one of the differences. The biggest difference is that I'm Jewish."

Muri shrugged. The word meant nothing to him. Danny tried again.

"That's my religion, Muri. You believe in Alchera right?"

The Aborigine nodded.

"Well, I believe in...different things."

"No matter. I teach you," Muri assured him.

"No, you don't understand. I can't learn. That is, I'm interested, of course, in what you believe in. But my beliefs don't leave room for other beliefs."

Muri stood up and kicked at a stone. "You no want to be my brother?" he asked, sounding like a five-year-old.

"I want to be your friend," Danny quickly answered, changing the subject. "You see, Muri, I have a family. We live in another country, not Australia. It's called America. Across the seas, far away." Danny saw the blank look on Muri's face and realized his friend had no idea what he was talking about. So he tried a different line.

"In America I live in a big city called New York. I go to

school. I have my mother and father. I live with them. You see, Muri, white people live together in families even when they're almost men."

"I teach you to live like man, like black man. You learn to make gunyah. Eat grubs," he insisted.

Danny could see that Muri had made up his mind. He had only one card left to play.

"Muri, if you don't get me back to the hotel soon, John and Rebecca and the *police* will come looking for me. You know what that means. They're probably looking for me right now!"

"They not come here," Muri said, as though reassuring Danny.

"Here tribal lands. Black men kill them."

"Muri, please," Danny pleaded. "In the morning, we must start going back. You take me, and I promise nothing will happen to you. I'll tell them we got lost."

"I never get lost," Muri said indignantly. "I just go walkabout. This my land."

"I know this is your land, Muri," Danny said, trying one last time to persuade him. "But that's just the point. It's your land, not mine. I don't want it. I don't want it at all, Muri. I'm just a tourist looking at your land. But I don't want to live here. Never! Can't you understand me, Muri?"

For the first time, Danny saw a glimmer of understanding in his friend's eye. But before Muri could answer, an ear-splitting noise rent the night. It was a half-human, half-animal cry that escalated into an ear-splitting roar.

Muri crouched in terror. "It's Nalja coming for me," he screamed.

Danny trembled. He remembered the story Barney, the old prospector, had told him at Coober Pedy about Nalja, the spirit of an old, old man with white hair, whose voice came from the hair beneath his armpits. If you saw him, you'd die.

Muri made little whimpering noises of fear, moving away from the fire and crawling into the shelter of the gunyah.

"Are you sure?" Danny asked, his teeth chattering.

"I sure. He come!" Muri screamed, pointing toward the desert. The dying embers of the fire sent strange shadows dancing on the ground in front of them. Another roar pounded their ears as they realized that Nalja, or whatever it was, was coming closer.

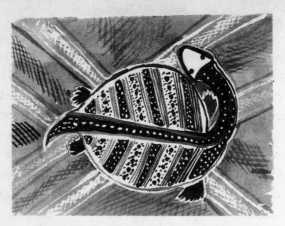

CHAPTER TEN

For the first time in many years, Danny began to cry.
When Muri heard Danny's muffled sobs, he came out of the
gunyah, despite his own terror.

"I no let him kill you," Muri assured Danny. "He kill me
first. You hide," he commanded and began running toward
the roar. In his right hand was a big rock, which he held
above him, ready to throw. Shouting his own war cry, Muri
charged. Danny watched him until he disappeared behind a
formation of boulders.

Suddenly, as if on command, the roaring stopped, along
with Muri's war cry. In their stead, Danny heard excited
words he couldn't make out and what sounded like laughter.

While Danny was debating whether to follow his friend, Muri returned, followed by a huge, fierce-looking black creature. The creature's body had yellow stripes, and his nose and chin were blood red. As the creature came near, Danny could see that it had wings of enormous feathers. On the creature's back was what looked like a giant cone-shaped mouth out of which swung a long black tail.

Nalja! was Danny's last thought as his mind short-circuited, and he fell down in a heap.

Danny awoke moments after he hit the ground. His first sight was Muri leaning over him, but the towering monster hovering over his friend convinced Danny that Nalja had indeed come to seek revenge for their trespassing on sacred ground.

Using his last ounce of strength, Danny lifted himself up on his elbows and prepared to make a run for it. But it was no use. He had no more strength left.

Muri seemed to read Danny's mind. "No 'fraid Danny. This my yagoo, Jajjala."

Danny vaguely recalled the word "yagoo." It had something to do with bones, or was that another word? Slowly, his mind relaxed, and he remembered Grant telling him about Muri's yagoo, his brother-in-law who'd put the bone through his nose and was helping him to "become a man."

Jajjala was smiling broadly. "Muri pass test," he explained, extending his hand to Danny. Jajjala, who Danny realized must be the husband of Nyan who worked at the hotel, looked about nineteen. His appearance was very scary, but now Danny could make out the ocher paint and feather hand bands attached to Jajjala. A loudspeaker hung from a rope on his back, and a long black wire extended from it.

Danny sat up and wiped his eyes. As he stood up, with the help of Muri, he asked nervously, "What was that terrible noise?"

Muri pointed to the loudspeaker. "Not Nalja. This *kalligooroo*," he whispered. At Danny's blank look, he explained, "Kalligooroo sacred. Not allowed to say name if women around."

Danny was certain that there were no other human beings, let alone women, within miles. Still he also whispered, "What's a kalligooroo?"

Jajjala answered, "This bull-roarer. Not blow to make noise, you just whirl it. Plenty frighten. Sometimes boy die of fright. But Muri brave. He ready to kill old Nalja. He pass test. He *balleli* now," he said proudly, his arm around Muri's shoulders.

Danny guessed that this meant Muri had gone another step higher in his initiation tests toward manhood. He was ashamed of his own temporary cowardice and very grateful that Muri, despite his terror, had rushed out to meet danger in order to protect him.

"Muri's very brave," he agreed.

Jajjala handed the bull-roarer to Muri. "You keep now," he told him. "But always hide from women or you die."

Danny thought there were a lot of taboos involved in being an Aborigine, but Muri seemed to take them in stride. Suddenly, Danny realized that here was a person who might be able to help him get back.

"Jajjala," Danny said hesitantly, "I have to go back to the hotel — where your wife, Nyan, works. Will you take me now? Muri wants to go walkabout, but I can't go with him. People are worried about me."

Jajjala was silent. Danny was desperate. "I must go back. Please help me."

"Not easy. You on sacred tribal lands now," he explained.

"Yes, I know," Danny said, weighing his options. He didn't want to betray his friend, especially since he had been prepared to put his life at risk for him, but what other choice was there? He was sure that even with Muri's help he would, sooner or later, succumb to the elements or meet some tragic end. He was a city boy, not some wild Aborigine with perfected survival instincts.

"Muri tricked me," Danny blurted out. "I didn't know. I didn't mean to trespass where white people can't go. I wanted to go back much earlier, but he wouldn't let me."

Rather than show any sympathy, Jajjala replied, "Spirits not let you go back till you one of us!"

"But I can't be like you!" Danny shouted, realizing that his feelings of fear were beginning to overwhelm him again. "It's not possible!"

Jajjala ignored the panic in his voice. "I take you and Muri to *corroboree*. We go now. Near here. Not far."

Danny knew he had no choice. There was no point in alienating his two protectors. "What's a corroboree?" he asked Muri, who was examining the bull-roarer and happily whirling it every now and then. The loudspeaker emitted small blasts of noise that echoed through the night. A bit like a *grager* on Purim, Danny thought to himself, which kids whirl to make a noise that will drown out the name of the wicked Haman. I wonder if they use the speaker to drown out the name of Nalja.

"Corroboree great. You like," Muri assured him, taking his arm and propelling him forward. Jajjala threw handfuls of dirt to put out the campfire. "Many men come," Muri told him. "We dance all night. Dance around our magic totems, like birds and animals in Alchera, the Dreamtime. Special. You like much," he emphasized.

Despite his fears, Danny felt excited. He was certain that no other white man had ever seen a corroboree. This would be a special experience. If he'd wanted adventure when he came to the Back of Beyond, this was his chance. And, after all, it was only one night...

CHAPTER ELEVEN

"Let's call the police," Rebecca implored.

"I think it best if we talk to Grant and his father first and get their advice," John replied. He blamed himself for letting Danny go with Muri against his better judgment. But the boy had been so persuasive, and Muri was someone John was sure could be trusted. But when Danny hadn't returned by nightfall, John realized there was something wrong.

They found Mr. Evans and his son in the hotel office. Grant couldn't understand their panic.

"He'll be okay with Muri," he assured them. "Safe as houses!"

"How do you know?" Rebecca asked.

" 'Cause Muri never gets lost. He often goes walkabout. All the Abos do. It's in their blood like."

"Well, how long does he usually stay away?" Rebecca pressed.

Grant was thoughtful. "Sometimes it's just a few days. Once it was a month. But nobody knows the bush better than Muri."

"Good heavens," John replied. "Danny can't stay in the bush until Muri's wanderlust runs its course. Muri might survive, but Danny won't."

"Not true," Mr. Evans interjected. "He's a good boy, Muri. If Danny's his friend, he'll look out for him and protect him — get him food and water. He's a bit lazy when it comes to work, but if it was my Grant with him, I wouldn't worry too much."

"That's all very well," John said shortly. "But Danny is my responsibility. I think I'd better follow Rebecca's suggestion and call the police."

"Don't do that!" Mr. Evans said, almost shouting. "Muri works for me and his sister, Nyan, is the best girl I've ever had to manage the souvenir shop. They're honest and smart and have never been any trouble. Bringing in the police will give them and their clan a bad name, not to mention what it will do to the hotel. There must be another way."

"Nyan!" Rebecca said excitedly. "I'll bet Muri's sister

will be able to tell us what to do."

"But she's not here now. She's gone home," Mr. Evans pointed out. "She finished work at five, almost three hours ago."

"Well, either we go to her home or to the police," John asserted, a no-nonsense look on his otherwise calm face.

"I don't know where it is," Mr. Evans admitted sheepishly. "Most of the Aborigines here live in shanties, on a kind of reservation. All the huts look the same," he added, a note of hopelessness in his voice.

"I know where Muri lives," Grant announced. "Been there lotsa times to visit him."

"I thought I told you not to go..." Mr. Evans started to say, but then thought better of it. "I'll get the car," he said, moving toward the door.

"Naw," his son said. "Ain't no road where Nyan lives. Quicker to walk."

Without another word, the four of them set out briskly. John and Rebecca were surprised how cold it had become in contrast to the blistering daytime heat. The cool breeze blew sand around them, stinging their eyes. Rebecca thought of her younger brother lost in the night, and her eyes began to fill with tears. Because he was a boy, he always acted tough, but she knew he would be scared. John, who knew how dangerous the terrain could be, had visions of Danny trapped under a fallen log or drowned in a water hole. A cold shiver ran down his spine.

At last they came to a clearing with a few tin buildings. Grant led them past these houses to a different section that had a collection of tumbledown, paper-bark shanties, which the Aborigines called "humpies." He made straight for the first one, very primitive, with the door barely hanging from the hinges. When they knocked, it almost fell off altogether.

Nyan came to the door. When she saw their serious faces, her initial smile melted into a look of panic. Her first thought was that money must be missing from the shop, but when she saw Rebecca and John, she realized it was something even more serious than that.

She backed away from the door and led them inside. The room looked like it had been robbed by professional thieves. The only furniture was a mattress, two wooden chairs and a rickety table with a lamp on it. Nyan's clothes must have been in the small, battered suitcase against the wall.

Nyan insisted that the men take the two chairs. She remained standing, while Grant and Rebecca squatted on the floor.

"Nyan, this really has nothing to do with you." Mr. Evans began, "It's just that we need your help."

Nyan just stared at him. She kept wondering if they had made some sort of mistake. After all, how could she help white people? She had no money.

Rebecca couldn't wait for the niceties to be over. "Do you know where Muri is?" she blurted out.

"Sure," Nyan said, relieved that was all they wanted.

"Where is he?"

"He go walkabout."

"Do you know exactly where?" John asked.

Nyan waved vaguely in the direction of the Olgas.

"Muri took Danny with him," Grant explained. "We're worried because they've been gone a long time, almost twelve hours. Danny was to be home before dark."

Nyan smiled, showing a flash of white teeth. "Twelve hours — you worry?" Nyan obviously thought that was ridiculous.

"When will they be back?" John demanded, losing his patience. "Muri come back few days," she answered a little nervously. She did not like this tall Aussie. "He be okay. Nearly man," she added.

Rebecca tried a different tack. "I'm sure your brother is fine, Nyan. He knows this country. But my brother, Danny, is not used to it. We come from a big, big city. He'll be hungry and thirsty, cold and tired." Her eyes filled with tears.

Nyan patted Rebecca on the shoulder. "Muri look after him," she assured her. "He good boy. Plenty food in the bush. No problem if he with Muri."

John was obviously not reassured. "This is getting us nowhere," he said, looking coldly at Nyan. "Where's your husband? Perhaps he can help us."

"Jajjala not here," she mumbled, her eyes to the ground.

"Will he be back soon?" John asked, looking at his watch.

"Few days — maybe week."

"Don't tell me he's gone walkabout, too!" Mr. Evans exclaimed, realizing that if they did not find Danny soon, John would surely go to the police.

"He go meet Muri," she told him. She did not feel comfortable telling them about the test her husband had planned for Muri. Somehow she felt this would get them both into trouble.

"So he knows where they are!" John said almost accusingly. "He track him. He find," she whispered, intimidated by John's tone of voice.

"Why is he doing that if Muri's okay?" Mr. Grant asked her.

"Not woman's business. I not supposed to know," she answered.

"Please," Rebecca implored, tears pouring down her face. "Please help us."

Nyan couldn't quite understand what the fuss was all about. Danny looked big and strong. Surely he would be able to handle a few days in the bush. But when she saw Rebecca crying, she decided that it was best to try and help them.

Nyan spoke very slowly. "Jajjala, my husband, he Muri's yagoo. That mean he helping Muri to become a man. He track him and make him pass test. Time for him to be balleli now."

"What's all this mumbo jumbo got to do with anything?" John asked, standing up. Mr. Grant put a restraining hand on his arm. He could see that Nyan was very reluctant to talk about it.

"He follow Muri," she continued, more afraid to stop than to go on. "Pretend he old Nalja. Frighten him to see if he brave."

"Good heavens. Who is old Nalja?" asked Mr. Evans.

"That's not important," Rebecca said, wiping her eyes. "What's important is that we get a message to your husband to bring Danny home — now. Tonight!"

"I not supposed to know. This man's business."

"Well, now it's our business," John said sharply. "Danny's not a man. He's just a kid. It might be okay for your brother to run around in the bush, but I'm responsible for Danny's safety. If I have to call in the police and put you all in jail for kidnapping, by God, I'll do it!"

"He be okay," Nyan said, her face a mask of terror again as she heard the word "police". "Muri brave. My husband no let anything bad happen."

Rebecca, despite her own fears, tried to comfort her. "Nyan, you're probably right. It's just that Danny's not even thirteen yet, and maybe he'll be frightened. Please help us. We don't want to call in the police, but he must be returned. Tonight!"

John whispered to Mr. Evans, "Perhaps she wants money. How much should I offer her to bring him back?"

Mr. Evans shook his head. "This can't be solved with money. She's got everything she needs — more than her sisters. I pay her well, too. Money's no use to an Aborigine out here in Back of Beyond. Look around you. What's she going to do with it? Listen, if her husband's tracking them, he'll make sure that they're safe. I know him. He's very savvy. I wouldn't be surprised if he brings him back tomorrow. He knows we'll be worried, and the last thing any of them want is for the police to start messing around."

But John was still worried. "Tomorrow then. It's too late for anyone to search for them now. If they're not back then, I'm going to the police."

Mr. Evans looked relieved. If Danny didn't show up tomorrow, he would be the one to call the police. It would look better for the record. He'd never lost a tourist to the bush, and he wasn't about to start now.

Rebecca was wondering if perhaps she should be calling the police herself. But she knew John was a responsible adult. On the other hand, he might be too embarrassed to call the police, since Danny was his responsibility. And yet, from what everyone was saying, her brother was being well taken care of.

As she reviewed the situation in her mind, Rebecca nervously fingered her opal necklace and saw Nyan's admiring look. In the semi-darkness, it was beautiful, seeming to emit blue fire from its milky depths. Rebecca loved it — it was her most treasured possession — but she loved Danny more.

"You can have it," she said to Nyan, "as soon as you bring my brother safely back to us."

CHAPTER TWELVE

Danny tagged along behind Jajjala and Muri, spurred on by his fear of being left behind. Although Jajjala had said the camp was nearby, they seemed to be walking for miles. The two Aborigines kept up a pace that was hard for Danny to follow. Fortunately, whenever he fell too far behind or stumbled, Muri was there to help him, as though he had eyes in the back of his head. Now that Danny had stopped demanding to be taken back to the hotel, Muri was in high spirits.

Danny felt a mixture of excitement and dread at the prospect of witnessing a corroboree. He tried to remember what he'd read in his magazine, *Habitat*. He knew it was some kind of pseudo-religious ritual, unchanged through thousands of years, probably steeped in witchcraft and sorcery. He imagined hundreds of black men pounding on tom-toms, uttering deep-throated chants and gyrating wildly around a bonfire. Yet, despite his visions of pagan rituals, he was excited at the prospect of experiencing what very few outsiders in the world had ever been invited to share.

Just when Danny felt that he couldn't walk another step, Jajjala stopped under a large gum tree. At first it looked to Danny the same as all the other eucalyptus trees, until he saw Jajjala put his hands inside it. Magic? he thought. Then he realized that the trunk had been hollowed out. Jajjala pulled out some boards that had been carved to look like animals.

"Them sacred," Muri informed him excitedly. "This hiding place called *beega*. If women find them, we have to kill them," he explained in a matter-of-fact voice.

Danny was horrified. "Even if they don't mean to — if it's an accident?"

"Sure," Muri said, smiling. "But if they don't see them, just walk under tree, spirits punish them. They get paralyze. No can walk anymore."

"What about white boys?" Danny asked nervously.

"Boys okay. White, black, no matter. You no worry."

In addition to the boards, which Danny could now see were crudely carved to represent different animals like liz-

ards, snakes and owls, plus an assortment of animal-like
things Danny had never seen before, Jajjala pulled out
strings of fur that he placed around Muri's waist, a necklace that seemed to be fashioned out of some kind of
animal's teeth and some other items Danny couldn't iden-
tify. He handed a strip of fur and a necklace to Danny, too.

Just like dressing up for Purim, Danny thought to himself. He knew what his costume would be the next time the
holiday came around.

Jajjala motioned for them to remove their shirts. Muri
did it eagerly; Danny, hesitantly. Jajjala began to paint
their bodies with charcoal and grease in a stripe pattern.
He then placed a band of possum fur on their heads. Danny
started to laugh until he saw how seriously Muri was taking it. Finally, Jajjala put a blob of red ocher on their
foreheads, cheeks and chests. Carrying the sacred boards,
he beckoned them to follow.

The bush suddenly came alive. Where there had been
utter silence except for bird calls and the occasional laugh
of the *kookaburra*, Danny could now hear the tramping of
many feet and muted words he could not understand coming from between the nearby clump of trees. They emerged
into a clearing where totem poles had been set up. There
were crowds of Aborigines, decorated in a manner similar
to their own.

"*Balgei! Balgei!*" the men shouted as a boy, who appeared to be a few years older than Muri, was led into the clearing. Many men rushed to meet him, bearing gifts of animal skins, vegetables, meat and woven baskets.

"What's balgei?" Danny whispered to Muri.

"He now ready to be man," Muri told him, unable to take his eyes off the young man. "Last test. Big party. Corroboree. Singing, dancing, feast. Then..." he hesitated.

"Then what?" Danny asked, not liking the way Muri hesitated.

"You see," Muri told him, patting him on the shoulder. "Very important. Big party. He soon be man."

The boy was placed on a decorated tree stump, like a king on a throne, in the center of a double circle drawn on the ground with a stick. Hordes of men, including Jajjala, surrounded him, raising their boomerangs in salute.

"His name Juginji," Muri told Danny. "Corroboree in his honor. Another year — maybe two — I also balgei."

Danny was happy that all the attention was centered on Juginji. No one seemed to notice that he was white. He realized that, like Muri, they probably didn't care, but it made him uneasy. Suddenly they lifted Juginji in the air for everyone to see. A murmur of approval swept the crowd. When they put him down again, everyone began to circle him singing what sounded like:

Wai-ung arree ngow,
wai-ung arree ngow,

Jandoo ngarrie ngaiee,
Wai-ung arree ngow.

These words were sung over and over again. Muri and Jajjala joined in the singing. The rhythmic beat and the repetition made Danny feel like singing, too. But he was too self-conscious for that.

Instead, Danny concentrated on the sight before him. In addition to carrying boomerangs, the men were all armed with spears. Their faces and bodies were painted in symbolic designs that made them look fiendish and fantastic. They looked like a war party about to embark on a raid.

A group of men broke through the circle around Juginji and took him away. The rest of the men arranged themselves in groups, forming several concentric circles. Then they joined together, each group moving in the opposite direction of the group in front of it. The glistening, painted black bodies were stamping, wheeling and swinging hypnotically. At the same time, they emitted loud, shrill noises that under ordinary circumstances Danny would have been hard pressed to call singing.

Without warning, the singing stopped as a double row of men lay flat on the ground with their heads in opposite directions. Another double row lay on top of them. Then another and another until there was a stack of bodies several feet high. Juginji climbed on top of this human mound as they began to rock and sway from side to side. At some unseen signal, the men jumped to their feet, letting Juginji fall gently into their midst. Then the dancing began in earnest.

Muri took Danny's hand and dragged him into a row of boys. Except for the clothing, or lack of it, it feels like a Hassidic wedding, Danny thought to himself, remembering the spirited dancing he'd once joined in at a cousin's wedding. The chanting became louder as the dancers stamped their feet. Juginji was lifted onto the shoulders of his yagoo. Then he was thrown into the air again and again by different groups of men.

At another hidden signal, the dancing abruptly stopped, and everyone sat down. From their woven baskets the men brought out their food and began to eat. To his great surprise, Danny found himself enjoying the ceremony. His fears were gone as he saw everyone was willing to accept him. No one looked at him strangely or treated him any differently from the Aboriginal boys.

For a moment, Danny played with the idea of really becoming Muri's brother. Now that would be something to tell his friends back home. He fantasized about the adventures he and Muri would have and how he would introduce his half-clad friend as "blood brother" to the bewildered faces of family and friends. Of course, it would be hard on Muri. Going "walkabout" in the city could be more dangerous than in the bush, and he couldn't really picture Muri in a suit and tie walking with him to synagogue on *Shabbat*.

On the other hand, what if he stayed here? Of course, that would be so much easier. No more school. No need to waste years at university. He could work a bit, like Muri did, and go walkabout whenever he felt like it. Dress up to look fierce, hunt animals, live in a gunyah in the Back of Beyond, watch the golden sun rise over Uluru every morning and, at the end of a hard day playing and hunting, he could sleep out in the open, under the stars, with his trusty spear and his friend at his side.

Of course, this might put a bit of a damper on his parent's Bar Mitzvah plans. Nor was he sure he was ready to go off on his own again. And, of course, there was the blazing sun and freezing nights...and...

Slowly, his daydream melted away, as reason and reality took over.

"You want vegetable food?" Muri asked him. "I bring."

An enormous amount of food was spread out on the ground. Apart from bowls of berries and nuts, there was nothing he recognized. Muri came back with a bowl filled with yams.

"Same I cook," he assured him. "No meat. Just roots throw in fire."

Danny was hungry. He softly said the appropriate blessing, which, more than any other time in his life, brought him to the realization of who he was. For him this was just a game, an enjoyable interlude before returning back to real life. But for those around him this was real life, a life he could not and should not be part of.

He began to eat the soft, yellow yams. They tasted delicious. Then he drank some kind of fruit juice and ate a bowl of berries and nuts. This was wonderful. Occasionally Jajalla would come over to see that he and Muri had food.

I wish I had a yagoo, Danny thought. Someone to always look out for me, like my own bodyguard. He caught himself daydreaming again but quickly stopped letting his mind wander.

I am me, he admonished himself. I'm a Jewish kid about to have a Bar Mitzvah. I don't need a private bodyguard. God looks out for me, but I do need a soft bed and a roof over my head. And I need my parents.

When the men had eaten and drunk their fill, a big fire was lit. The men placed thick green logs on it, and dense smoke billowed out. Armed with their hunting weapons, they danced into the middle of the smoke.

"This restore their strength," Muri whispered to Danny, nudging him to dance into the smoke with him. Danny followed Muri's lead, but he kept coughing as the smoke burned his nostrils. He was desperate to sit down but didn't want to insult anyone.

Each person performed a strange kind of dance on the logs burning in the fire, jumping in and then out again indifferent to the flames that were licking the logs. As the smoke slowly died away, the last boy jumped off the logs.

As the morning star became visible, the Aborigines sang another song, and then the younger boys sang what Muri said was the kingfisher song. The kingfisher bird was one of the clan's totems. Boys who were not yet initiated as men began to climb an old gum tree, using just their hands and bare feet, swinging from the branches and then falling to the ground.

"Aie! Aie!" the older men cried as each boy landed safely. "What does it mean?" Danny asked Muri after he'd also climbed, landed and returned to his side.

"This from Alchera, the Dreamtime, when men were birds and birds were men."

"Is the corroboree over now?" Danny asked, barely suppressing a yawn.

Muri avoided his eyes. "Not over. Main part begin now," he admitted uncomfortably. "First the fun — now serious part."

As Danny looked around, he saw that everyone around him was seated, as though expecting some major event. The excitement that had filled him began to ebb away. The whole atmosphere was changing before his eyes. There was tension in the air, and some of the younger boys glanced hesitantly toward Juginji, who was coming toward the middle of the circle. Juginji himself suddenly looked older, more mature and, although Danny was sure no Aborigine would admit it, just a little bit scared.

It was the calm before the storm, except that even the calm seemed laced with the scent of fear!

CHAPTER THIRTEEN

The sun began to rise over Uluru, which was still visible in the distance through the trees. The air felt hot and humid. The sky was not red, as it had been most mornings, but filled with low, threatening, dark clouds.

"Wet begin soon. Few days," Muri confided to Danny, who remembered the old prospector Barney telling him that there were only two seasons in Back of Beyond: "the wet and the dry." Yet, despite the almost tropical heat, Danny was shivering.

All the boys who had taken part in the tree ceremony, including Muri, formed a group, and a witch doctor began to dance in front of them. Then a group of older men tore strips of paper bark from a tree and made a long belt, tying the ends with fur around Juginji's waist. He was told to lie down, and for the first time, there was no mistaking the look of fear in his eyes. The men tied string tightly around the boy's lower arms until their veins stood out. Then, in a swift motion, each boy took out a knife and pierced their veins. Holding their arms over Juginji, the boys let their blood rain down upon Juginji until his face and body were entirely covered with blood.

Danny looked at the scene in front of him and, for a brief second, thought that perhaps they were all playing a trick on him. Maybe this is all pretend, like the test Jajjala gave Muri, he wondered. But then the smell of the blood and the silent look of pain on the young boys' faces brought Danny back to reality.

"No," he heard himself saying. "No! I can't look at this. They're savages. How can they do this disgusting thing?" Then he thought of running away. Perhaps he could hide until daylight. Surely someone would come looking for him.

As though reading his mind, Muri came back to Danny and, with blood still on his forearms, took Danny's hand and held him tightly. Before he could say anything, the next, more terrible stage of the initiation began.

Trying not to look but unable to turn away, Danny watched the men nearest Juginji begin to sit down in some prearranged order. Muri whispered the words *"jamung-ungur"* to Danny. When Danny turned to him with a blank look, he said two words that sent an involuntary shudder down Danny's spine: "Blood drinking!"

By now the men had formed two circles. The inner circle consisted of male relatives of Juginji. His father sat right next to him. Juginji stretched himself out on the ground with his head on his father's thighs. Then the relatives rose and began dancing. One after another they stepped over Juginji's head while his father covered his son's eyes.

"If he look," Muri told Danny, "both his mother and father die."

"I want to go now," Danny moaned softly. "Please. I don't want to watch this. Take me away."

But Muri ignored him. Danny knew that if Muri let go of his arm he might collapse right there in front of everyone. A cold sweat broke out on his face, and he looked down at his own brightly painted body with loathing.

"I'm no better than they are," he told himself. "I'm a pagan! An idol worshipper! How could I have let this happen?"

A wooden vessel was placed near one of Juginji's uncles. "He Juginji's mother's brother," Muri whispered. Danny watched in horror as Juginji's uncle repeated the blood-letting ritual. He tied his arm, and when the veins seemed about ready to burst out of his arm, he took a small bone, similar to the ones in the men's noses, and pierced a vein, letting the blood pour into the vessel. His uncle then passed the bone to the next man who duplicated the procedure. Each man in succession poured his blood into the vessel until the wooden bowl was full to overflowing.

The vessel was brought to Juginji as his father uncovered the boy's eyes. Then, his father put his hands around the boy's throat as if to strangle him. Danny looked at Muri, terrified.

"Stop him throwing up when he drink," Muri explained, shuddering a little himself as the crude, blood-filled chalice was held to Juginji's lips. But Danny didn't wait to see him drink. Breaking out of Muri's grip, he half-stumbled, half-crawled to the back of some bushes, as waves of nausea overcame him. The words he had been studying for his Bar Mitzvah thundered in his head:

> *And you shall eat no manner of blood, whether it be of fowl or of beast in any of your dwellings. Whosoever it be that eats any blood, that soul shall be cut off from his people.*

Maybe it's too late, Danny thought, his mind reeling. Maybe the things I've witnessed tonight have already cut my soul off from my people. Jews are forbidden to eat the blood of animals. How much more terrible to drink human blood! He felt flushed and ill. But his thoughts wouldn't stop. Have I become an idol worshipper? Is joining in idolatry like idolatry itself? Didn't I enjoy the ceremony? Didn't I — even if it was for just a moment — imagine that I could be part of all this?

In that moment, lying in the bushes, feeling nauseous and disgusted with himself, Danny fought what he would years later call his battle for his soul. Like his forefather Jacob, who wrestled with the angel without a name and won, so too Danny wrestled with the thousands of unnamed desires and yearnings that boys dream about and long for — and won. And like Jacob, who received a new name and a new identity by virtue of his triumph, so Danny felt himself change and evolve into a new person, one who was ready to become part of a heritage and a nation that his parents had prepared for him. This new Danny looked down at his half-naked body, and for the first time in a long time, he felt shame.

Then, picking himself up, he started to walk back to Muri. I am not an idol worshipper, he declared to himself. I didn't do this willingly, and I didn't eat forbidden food, and I didn't drink any blood. But that doesn't mean I'm out of danger. Until I get out of here, anything can happen. But I have to try and remain calm, he told himself, and now that I know this ceremony has no power over me, I have to do whatever it takes — short of actual idol worship — to get out of here.

Danny recalled his Torah teacher's words: "There are three commandments for which a Jew must die rather than transgress. Remember them:

ONE — the commandment not to kill;

TWO — the commandment against immorality;

THREE — the commandment against idol
worship.

"If a Jew is forced to transgress all the other commandments on pain of death, under circumstances that don't publicly defame the Jewish religion, he may transgress to save his life. Why? Because the Torah says, 'And you will live by them!' That means the commandments were given for you to live by, and, more important, they are designed for the living. If you have to give up a commandment in order to live, even if you have to transgress the Shabbat, then you may do so. Only these three transgressions are inviolate. Remember."

"It's funny what you remember when you need to," he said out loud as he saw Muri coming to meet him.

CHAPTER FOURTEEN

Danny was surprised to see Muri accompanied by a smaller boy, whom, he was sure, hadn't been at the corroboree.

"He my little brother, Moonnup," Muri said, indicating the boy, who was studying Danny with such a mature, serious expression that for a second Danny thought the boy was a midget. On closer inspection, Danny saw that the boy was about eight. He was short and chubby in his shorts and shirt, which barely closed across his fat tummy. "He bring message from Nyan."

"Your sister?" Danny asked, feeling that his ordeal might now be over.

Muri nodded, shifting from one foot to the other.

"What message? Are we going home now?" Danny asked eagerly.

"She say I have to bring you back. She woman. No can tell me what to do," he said defiantly.

Danny almost laughed to himself. He had a mental picture of himself saying to his sister, "You no can tell me what to do," and her being ready to strangle him. Obviously, women's lib had not yet reached the Aborigine people.

"Listen, Muri, we're friends, aren't we?"

"More. Want you be my brother," Muri said with sadness in his voice.

"But I can't be your brother, Muri, although I really do like you. I will be your friend for always. And anyway, it's probably not your sister who is asking that you take me back — it's probably John or the police. Now you don't want the police to come here, do you? You don't want to go to jail?"

"No afraid," Muri answered dejectedly.

"I'm not saying you're afraid," Danny continued, realizing he had to develop a new approach. "But if you don't take me back, my family will never let me come here again, and we'll never get a chance to see each other. If you take me back right away, I'll explain everything. And who knows? Maybe one day you'll be able to come and visit me in my country."

Muri brightened up noticeably when Danny talked about his visiting the States.

"We've got all sorts of things in my country you don't have here. We have Disney World, where you go on rides and see all sorts of wonderful things. We have the tallest buildings in the world. We even have mountains taller than Uluru!"

"No rock bigger than Uluru. Uluru sacred," Muri insisted. Danny sensed he wasn't getting through.

"You know," he said quietly, "in my religion, we are taught that you don't do to other people what you wouldn't want them to do to you. That means, if someone doesn't want to be in a place, you shouldn't force him to be there, understand?"

"What I do to you? I not look after you?" Muri said angrily.

"Yes, yes, of course you did," Danny backtracked, not wanting to make Muri feel he was ungrateful, and yet not wanting his friend to think that what he was doing was right. "You were kind and brave, much braver than me. But Muri, you have taken me away from a people and a life that means a lot to me, more than being here. Please try and understand this."

Muri wouldn't look at him, but Danny knew he was listening.

"Look, let's say you came to visit my country. I'm sure

you would be frightened by New York, my city. It is big and noisy, and there are buildings they call skyscrapers, because they're so tall, they seem to touch the sky."

When Muri still didn't speak, Danny continued. "How would you feel if I told you that you had to stay there? You could never again see your people, your mother and father, brothers and sisters, your yagoo, again? Never see Uluru, or go to a corroboree, or walkabout, never hear any more stories about Alchera, the Dreamtime? What if I said you had to live in this city of mine forever and be my brother! Would you be happy?"

Muri shook his head slowly. There were a few painful moments of silence.

"I let you go back," Muri whispered sadly. Then, after a moment's thought, he said, "But you on sacred land now. If you not be my brother, they kill you," he warned.

Danny swallowed. Out of the frying pan...

"What would I have to do to be your brother?" he asked Muri. Perhaps he could just perform some simple ceremony.

"You mix your blood with ours. Then we let you dance around our totem. Maybe they want you to do things I do to become a man our people proud of. Then you come and go just as you like."

Blood. That was all Danny could think about: Having to undergo that terrible blood ceremony. Drinking blood.

"Muri, I can't do those things," he said desperately. "Isn't there another way?"

Muri closed his eyes, concentrating. Then he spoke rapidly to his little brother, who ran off. "I send him to get Jajjala," he explained. "Jajjala know what to do."

Muri looked so sad that Danny felt very sorry for him and wished he could think of a way to make him feel better. His friend had paid him a great compliment in wanting him for a brother, but they lived not only on different continents, but in different worlds.

Jajjala came, still looking fierce in his stripes and feathers, carrying his boomerang and spear. He and Muri spoke for quite a while in low tones, in their own language. Danny was unable to tell by the tone of their voices and their expressions what was being decided. Finally, it was Jajjala who spoke to him, kindly but with authority in his voice.

"It decided. You come back to corroboree now. We do an ancient dream dance, and we let you see the sacred and secret parts of the dance, forbidden to women. After that you talk of how you now friend of our tribe. You promise not to tell anyone our secrets ever. Then you eat bark of our *nala* tree. After that, Muri take you out of our sacred tribal lands — back to hotel."

Danny felt both elated and scared. "What are these 'sacred and secret parts'? Is this dance like the dance with blood? And if I promise not to tell, will they understand me?"

Jajjala only answered the last question. "You say in your language. Most understand. I also repeat in our tongue."

"What did you say I have to eat?" Danny asked nervously.

"I not know name you call it. But it bark of the nala tree. Taste good."

"No meat. No bugs," Muri added.

"And no blood?" Danny asked again.

This time Jajjala smiled. "Frighten you, our blood drinking?"

Danny nodded.

"Me, too, when I do it. But it make me a man, big warrior. After that, I marry Nyan. Not be afraid. Come!" he commanded, motioning Danny and Muri to follow him. Moonnup had already disappeared. Perhaps, Danny thought, he had gone back to tell everyone he was coming home soon.

Danny's legs were shaking. He still didn't have a clear picture of whether he would have to drink blood or not. Would they really kill him if he refused?

CHAPTER FIFTEEN

They went back to the clearing where the corroboree was being held. Many of the Aborigines had left, but some were still squatting on the ground, passing around food. Danny and Muri stood under the trees at the outskirts of the clearing, while Jajjala went and spoke to the old men of the tribe. The elders kept looking at Danny and shaking their heads. He felt glad that Muri was with him, but while his friend might protect him from demons like Nalja, would he — could he — protect him against his people?

One of the elders of the tribe held up his spear, and immediately there was silence. The thin, old man made some kind of an announcement, and all eyes turned to Danny. Then the men formed themselves into groups and began to

dance. Muri breathed a sigh of relief and whispered to
Danny, "This is the *Wanji-wanji*, the ancient dream dance."
As they danced, they sang the same words over and over
again:

Warri wan-gan-ye.

Koogunarri wanji-wanji.

Warri wan-gan-ye.

"What does it mean?" Danny asked Muri.

He shook his head. "Don't know. Only very old men remember. Maybe they tell me when I man."

While the words were rhythmic and repetitious, the
dance was very intricate. It started at a slow cadence, the
men's feet alternately shuffling and then lightly touching
the ground. As the tempo increased, the men seemed to fly
in the air, twirling around and around, in unison. Even the
old men joined in, their bird-like movements belying their
age. Unbelievably, the speed of the beating drums increased, as spears and boomerangs pierced the air above
the frenzied dancers, who were by now moving their feet in
what to Danny was a blur. For a brief moment, each person
was able to manage the complex steps until exhausted, and
one by one they slowed down, finally sinking to the ground,
as though in sleep.

The old man named Dhalja beckoned Danny to come
and stand in the center of the circle. All the men sat up,
and Danny could feel their unblinking eyes focused on him.

Goosebumps suddenly appeared on his skin, and the hair at
the back of his neck stood stiff. Jajjala came and stood beside him.

"Speak!" the old man commanded.

Danny's mind went blank. He couldn't remember what
to say. The more he looked at the old man's fiery eyes, and
at the sweat pouring down many of the dancers, the more
he began to feel afraid and alone. Then he felt Muri come
up from behind him and whisper, "No afraid. Speak your
heart."

That broke the spell that seemed to paralyze Danny.
He cupped his face in his hands for a moment, collected his
thoughts and began. "I...I...just want to say.... My name is
Danny. I come from a country a very long way away. It's
called America." There was total silence. Danny cleared his
throat.

"I am a visitor in Australia. I met your tribesman,
Muri. He became my friend — and protector," he added,
wanting somehow to express his thanks to his friend. "I
came walkabout with him, but I didn't know we crossed
into sacred tribal lands." He stopped.

Jajjala took his silence as a sign that he should trans-
late what Danny had just said. Meanwhile, Danny was
collecting his thoughts. When he had finished translating,
Jajjala nudged him to continue.

"I must return tomorrow to my own country. But I have

learned much from you and my friend Muri. Until I came here I had only heard of your wonderful land and the wonderful deeds that were done by your people. I had read about you, but I never really understood what I was reading. Now I do.

"I am proud that you have let me be part of your ceremonies and your history. I am proud that you have considered me worthy to be part of your lives. I know I don't know much about your ways, but I want you to know I am your friend and will be so forever."

Now Danny took a deep breath while Jajjala translated. He knew that what he had to say now was very important to the tribe and could possibly be the difference between life and death.

"I promise I will never tell anyone what I have seen here at this corroboree — not even my mother and father. These sacred things that I have seen here have been for my eyes alone. No one will hear of them from my lips. I promise you." His voice was shaking. He wanted to add, "But please don't make me drink any blood!" but he was too afraid.

The elders gathered together for a moment. There was a lengthy rumble of strange words and phrases, but it seemed to be friendly. Dhalja motioned to Muri to give something to Danny. He extended his hands, and Danny saw they were filled with a brown, papery substance.

"Eat," Muri whispered to him. "Not bad. Sweet."

Danny took a mouthful and found that it really was quite palatable — eating it was not that different from chewing a piece of sugar cane.

"*Yudu*," shouted the men.

"It means 'close your eyes'," Muri told him.

Danny hesitated. He remembered how Juginji's father had covered his eyes just before the blood-drinking ceremony.

"Close your eyes," Muri repeated urgently. "No make ceremony until eyes closed. Bad luck."

But what if they bring blood? Danny thought. What will I do? And what if they hold me by the throat like they did to Juginji and make me swallow the blood?

He began to sweat profusely. He wanted to run, to hide, but Muri and Jajjala were on either side of him, and he knew he was no match for either of them.

"No afraid, promise," Muri whispered through clenched teeth.

Danny closed his eyes. He tried to open them just a bit in the hope of seeing what would happen, but the sun was out, and it was hard to focus without opening his eyes more than a slit.

A high, flowing song emanated from in front of him. Muri told him to open his eyes. There, in front of him, an old man was holding a totem board perhaps fifteen feet high. He held it almost at shoulder length. It was carved and painted in white clay with dabs of red ocher. Danny couldn't understand why it didn't fall. At the same time the entire group had taken up the chant and began singing faster and faster.

"Song of kangaroo," Muri told him, shouting above the din. The men beat branches on the ground in rhythm with the words. Dhalja came forward and presented him with a small totem board, carved with circles, diamonds and squares.

"This hold all the mystery of life," Jajjala confided to Danny. He led him to a hollow tree, where he was instructed to place the totem board. Jajjala covered it with fresh leaves from the *mallee* tree, until it was totally hidden. Then the Aborigines filed past Danny, each one touching him on the shoulder with their spears as they passed.

A horrible-looking warrior, with wild, bloodshot eyes approached Danny. His painted face and body were so frightening that Danny cringed. In his hands was a long spear, with a sharpened stone for a blade. He raised his spear high above Danny's head and held it there, poised to plunge it into his victim.

Danny's voice dried up in his throat. He opened his mouth, but nothing came out. His heart was pounding, and when his eyes met the warrior's, they pleaded for mercy. But the man's face was like stone. Danny was certain he had failed the test or had seen something he was not allowed to see or, worse, had broken one of their myriad taboos. He realized that this man had been chosen to kill him, and that neither Jajjala nor Muri could help him. He could think of only one thing to do. Raising himself as tall as he could, he took a deep breath and shouted in Hebrew, singing with all his might, "Hear O Israel, the Lord our God, the Lord is one."

Suddenly, the man, still holding his spear up high, came face to face with Danny. He could feel the other's hot breath on his cheeks. Then the warrior broke into a toothless grin.

"Friend!" the man said in English, bringing his spear down gently and tapping its head on Danny's shoulder.

"Friend!" Danny mumbled, almost fainting in relief.

The warrior turned and walked back to the others. Another man came forward. He too tapped Danny's shoulder with his spear. One after another, each man tapped Danny's shoulder with his spear. When the last one had gone, Jajjala turned to Muri.

"You take him home now," he said. Then he asked Danny, "What those words? No hear white man talk like that before. Song nice. Maybe you teach me. Muri listen good. Pick up song quickly."

Danny thought about explaining, but decided against it. No need to reinforce the obvious: that he had been scared to death.

Instead he simply answered, "That's Hebrew, the ancient tongue of my people. I use a tune like that when I say my Bar Mitzvah portion of our Bible, our Torah. That was the *Shema*. We say it to give us strength, to make us mighty warriors, like you."

"Not work too good for you," Jajjala said with a smile, making it clear that he knew Danny had been scared. "Better you learn from Muri and me."

"It worked fine," said Danny, returning the smile. "Just fine."

CHAPTER SIXTEEN

For eight hours, the two boys trekked through the desert. To Danny, nothing looked familiar, and he marvelled at the way Muri seemed to know exactly where they were. Actually, had Muri been alone he would have made the trip in half the time, but he stopped numerous times to give Danny a chance to rest. He realized that while Danny might be his friend and tribal brother, he would never have been able to pass even the simplest Aborigine test of manhood.

It was almost sunset when they got back to the hotel. Moonnup had arrived much earlier with the news that Danny and Muri were on their way. Almost the entire hotel — everyone had heard rumors of Danny's disappearance —

gathered to welcome him back. Rebecca, Mr. Williams, Grant Evans and his father and Nyan were at the head of the procession.

"Danny!" Rebecca shouted when she saw him. Running at full speed she grabbed him in a bear hug and practically lifted him off the ground. "Danny!" she kept shouting, tears running down her face.

Danny had never seen his sister so concerned about him, and at first he didn't know how to react. He even thought something might have happened to their parents, the way she was carrying on. But when she said accusingly, "What happened? We were all so worried!" he knew that her concern had been for him alone.

John and the other men kept asking him if he was okay, to which he could only answer, "Sure." Now, in the safety of his friends and family, he felt more secure, and he wanted to tell them all what had happened. But he knew he could not do that, certainly not the whole story.

Muri stayed in the background, looking very uncomfortable. He thought it funny that the white man's tribe showed such concern just because they had gone walkabout. But he couldn't help but notice the angry stares some people were giving him. They seemed to be upset at him, but he couldn't understand why. Hadn't he watched over Danny, as he had promised? Hadn't he brought him back unharmed? And, anyway, they had only been gone two days, barely enough time to visit the clearing, and certainly far less time than his usual week-long jaunts. Yet what bothered him most was the fact that neither Grant nor his father had ever asked him where he had gone when he left for weeks at a time, and never, ever had they come to greet him — and he knew them much longer than Danny did!

Danny was also uncomfortable. People were staring at him as well. The reason was the stripes. He had buttoned his shirt right up to the top, but even so, the colored stripes on his arms were visible below the sleeves. He'd tried to wash them off, or at least smear the colors so that they would look like dirt, but instead the stripes looked like they had been tattooed on and dirt spread around them. His face, too, had traces of red ocher. Rebecca couldn't resist teasing him and said, "Wash up, you wild Indian!" which didn't make him feel any better about his appearance.

While Danny was being welcomed by the crowd, Nyan walked over to her brother and began questioning him, first in a whisper and then more loudly. Danny saw Muri look sheepishly down at the ground, and it reminded him of the numerous browbeatings he had received from *his* older sister. Around men, they're really macho, and girls don't count for much, he thought to himself, but in reality Muri gets pushed around by his older sister like any younger brother.

Finally, Muri raised his head, obviously trying to defend his actions. The only word that Danny could make out was the word corroboree, which came up several times. Grant picked up on it, too.

"Wow, you went to a corroboree?" he said to Danny. "What was it like? I didn't know white men were even allowed at a corroboree."

Grant ran over to Muri, grabbing the Aborigine's hand. "Muri, I want to go to a corroboree, too. When will you take me?" he almost whined.

A few people — native Australians — were obviously impressed when they heard that Danny had gone to a corroboree. They immediately converged on him, asking all sorts of questions about the ceremony. They especially wanted to know if, given the markings on Danny's arms and head, he had become a member of Muri's tribe.

John saw how uncomfortable all this was making both boys, and he decided to intervene. "That's enough questions for one day," he said, inserting himself between Danny and the knot of people who had suddenly converged on him.

"But this is unbelievable," Grant shouted above the voices of John and the crowd. "He may have been the first white man ever to witness a corroboree or actually be involved in one. C'mon, Danny, tell us what happened."

There was an embarrassing silence as everyone waited for Danny to speak. He was thinking of what to say when, suddenly, lightning lit up the sky, and water literally splashed down in waves upon them.

"The wet begin," Muri announced as everyone raced back to the hotel.

Danny didn't stop in the lobby. He raced to his room. John wasn't far behind him.

"Don't worry, Danny," John said. "I didn't tell your parents what happened, although I was going to if Nyan hadn't told us you would be coming back soon. I didn't want to worry them unless it was absolutely necessary. After all, what could they do so far away?"

"Thanks, John," Danny told him as he entered his room. "I appreciate it, and also what you did for me out there. But I've got to try and get this stuff off me," he said, holding out his arm, "and then we can talk more."

John nodded and returned to the lobby.

"We go now," he heard Nyan say as he left the elevator. She was pushing Muri toward the front door.

"I'll drive you," Mr. Evans offered.

"Is nothing. Just water. Rain not bother us." She shrugged, grabbing her brother and heading into the downpour.

"Wait, Nyan!" Rebecca yelled, following them into the rain. Dripping wet, she unclasped the opal necklace, giving it one last, loving look before handing it to Nyan. "This is yours — I promised," she said.

Nyan held it in the palm of her hand and seemed ready to take it. It radiated a shimmering blue fire, even in the rain. Each time the lightning struck, you could see all the colors of the rainbow reflected in the opal's milky depths.

"No, I not take it," she said softly, handing it back.

"But it's yours," Rebecca insisted. "I promised."

"I help bring back your brother not for this. I know plenty trouble to Muri if he no bring back your brother soon. I love my brother, too," she declared, giving Muri a gentle shove. He looked surprised, as though he was hearing this for the first time

"But you must have something, just to remember us by. I know..." Rebecca slipped off a dainty pinky ring she'd received for her *Bat Mitzvah*. It was a slender band of gold, set with a small freshwater pearl. Nyan wanted to protest again, but Rebecca took her hand and slipped it on the girl's little finger. There was an awkward moment of silence.

"I understand the Aborigines," John said, coming out of the hotel, "but I thought Americans had more sense than to stay out in the rain," he teased good-naturedly.

Rebecca leaned over and gave Nyan a peck on the cheek. Then she waved good-bye to Muri, and, together with John, she rejoined the others in the hotel.

Danny came down about half an hour later. He had managed to scrape off most of the ocher. Here and there were splotches of faded color that from close up made him look like he had a bad case of the chickenpox. The three of them sat in the corner as John prepared to go over the rest of their itinerary. Occasionally someone would come by and say "welcome back" to Danny. In a place where little changed from day to day, Danny had become a bit of a celebrity.

"We're leaving Uluru tomorrow," said John. "I'd like to make an early start. We'll have a few days in Sydney and Melbourne, just so you can say that you've seen the big cities, and then it's the long journey home. I suggest we all get a good night's sleep."

Danny was more tired than he thought. He put his head on the pillow and, after what seemed like only minutes, he was woken by knocking on his door.

"Rise and shine, as you Americans say," John's voice boomed out. "We let you sleep an extra hour. It's almost seven."

"Is that A.M. or P.M.?" Danny shouted from his bed.

He heard John chuckling. "That'll teach you to go walkabout!"

The first thing Danny did when he went downstairs was search for Muri.

"He's not here," Grant told him. "I think he was too embarrassed to come to work."

Undaunted, Danny ran outside to the pool. Grant was right. Muri was nowhere to be found. Dejected, he headed back to the hotel, only to discover that Muri was talking to Rebecca.

"Hi," Rebecca called out. "Where've you been? Muri and I were looking all over for you."

"I was looking for you guys," Danny said, although he actually meant he was looking just for Muri.

Rebecca sensed that the two boys wanted to be alone and excused herself, saying she was going to finish packing. "Which you'd better do also," she reminded him.

Once they were alone, Danny began speaking softly, in as reassuring a voice as he could muster.

"Muri, I know you must be nervous about me, but I want you to know that I would never say anything about the corroboree. I may never be one of you, or be able to pass even the easiest of your tests for manhood, but I will be your friend for life, and I'll never forget you or the experiences I had with your tribe."

Muri nodded.

"There's something I want to give to you. Wait here," Danny said.

He raced up to his room and came back, out of breath.

"You know what this is?" he asked Muri.

Muri looked at the cassette player and said, "This where your music come from. Grant's father let me use it sometimes when I work. I listen to the music."

"It's yours, Muri," Danny said proudly. "And there's a tape inside of the kind of music you said you liked when you heard me speak in my special tongue." Danny turned the machine on, and the sounds of his Bar Mitzvah portion filtered through the lobby.

"I know it by heart already," he confided. "Whenever you play it, remember me."

Muri took the cassette recorder with both hands, as if he was carrying something holy.

"This best totem of all," he told Danny. "I no let women hear it. They hear it, they die."

Danny hadn't expected that reaction. "Uh, no Muri. This totem can be seen and heard by everyone. In my country they call it an...an..." — he remembered seeing the words he was thinking of in *The New York Times* — "an equal-opportunity totem," he said, smiling. "Both men and women are permitted to hear it."

Muri nodded, but Danny could see how perplexed his friend was. How could a sacred totem be permitted to women?

In return, Muri took out a jar and gave it to Danny. It was the red ocher used to paint the faces and bodies of the men of his tribe. "For when you go walkabout," he told him.

"For when I go walkabout," Danny agreed, and held out his hand. Muri shook it.

"Good-bye, friend," Danny said.

"Good-bye," Muri answered. "I go finish tests. Be big man in tribe. Listen tape. Maybe learn be big man in your tribe, too."

Danny smiled as the Aborigine turned, clicked on the tape, put it to his ear and walked out, listening to the melodious sounds that Danny himself would soon be singing at his Bar Mitzvah.

CHAPTER SEVENTEEN

The Saturday morning of Danny's Bar Mitzvah celebration was sunny and crisp. His mother had been buzzing in and out of his room since dawn, arranging his clothes, trying to reassure him he would do just fine and, in general, making him nervous.

Danny put on his new suit, a white shirt, a blue-striped tie and a velvet *kippah*, with his name written on it in Hebrew on his head. As he looked in the mirror, he smiled to himself. Everything is relative. Compared to Muri's nine tests of manhood, I'm getting off easy.

On the other hand, he suddenly realized, *after* the Bar Mitzvah I've got 613 commandments to keep, and work at, plus umpteen years of religious schooling. When Muri finishes his tests, he is a man, and then the pressure is over. My tests of manhood, of being a good Jew, never stop. I get tested every day of my life. Hmm...maybe our way *is* harder....

He sat down at his desk and began to sing the opening passages of Tzav from the portion *VaYikra* (Leviticus), which he would shortly read in the synagogue in front of the whole congregation. There was a light tap at his door. "Come in," he said.

Rebecca came in, wearing a very pretty, lilac silk dress and the opal pendant she almost never removed.

"I must be dreaming," Danny said, looking stunned. "*You* actually knocked! You actually knocked *and* waited until I said, 'Come in.' I can't believe it."

Rebecca came over and squeezed his shoulder. "I'm glad you noticed. That's because, as the saying goes, 'today you are a man.'"

He grinned. "I wonder how long this newfound respect will last?"

"At least until lunchtime." They both laughed.

Rebecca walked around his room aimlessly, as though waiting for something. Danny didn't know what she wanted, and he certainly wasn't going to make it easy for her. He went back to his singing.

"Danny," she finally said, realizing he wasn't going to ask her what she wanted. "There's something I've been wanting to ask you," she continued, and then waited until he stopped singing and looked up. "I haven't really bothered you with it until now, because I get the feeling you're a little uncomfortable with the whole subject. But now that you're a man, and we're, well, sort of equals, I thought you might want to tell me if I promise not to tell anyone — not even Mom and Dad."

"I think I missed part of this conversation. What do you want me to tell you?"

"Come on, Danny, you know. I want you to tell me what happened during those two days you were missing with Muri."

Danny looked at his sister, and she could see he was weighing in his mind whether or not to tell her.

"So all this knocking and 'today you are a man' stuff was just to get something from me?"

"Of course not, Danny," she quickly said, sounding hurt. "You've matured a lot, especially since our trip, even without this Bar Mitzvah. You seem to have...grown up in here" — she pointed to her head — "and you're not half as babyish as you used to be."

"Thanks a lot," he said sarcastically, "but this sounds suspiciously like reverse psychology to me. And anyway, we went walkabout, that's all. Now would you mind letting me go over my Torah reading?"

Rebecca saw that Danny had made up his mind not to

tell her anything, but she had no intention of leaving. Not without a fight. "I talked to Nyan while you were gone, you know. She told me a little bit about the corroboree."

"She wouldn't know. Women aren't allowed to attend them. And if they do attend, you know what happens to them?" Danny asked, letting the question hang in the air for a moment. "They die!"

"Well, she may not have gone to one, but she heard things." This time it was Rebecca's turn to build up the suspense. She cleared her throat. "Blood! She said they have to drink human blood. She once overheard her husband talking to his father. They have to drink a whole cup of blood before they can be called a man."

Danny didn't answer.

Rebecca realized she was on the right track. "Did they make you do that? Did they, Danny? Did they hold you and force you to drink human blood? You can tell me, Danny."

He shook his head violently, avoiding her face. He recalled Juginji lying on the floor, with his father's hand around his neck and the vessel filling with blood. He shivered inadvertently.

"Danny, I'll understand, honest. I'm sure if you —"

"I didn't — I couldn't," he insisted.

"Okay," she said when she saw how agitated he had become. Rebecca didn't want to make him more nervous than he already was, but she couldn't help herself. She had to know.

"Did they make you do anything terrible?" she asked quietly.

"No, Rebecca, they didn't. Look, I can't tell you anything. I promised. That's also part of being a man and maturity — keeping your promises. They're sort of good people and I — "

"What do you mean, 'sort of'?" Rebecca interrupted.

Danny took a deep breath. This conversation was hard for him. Not for the reasons Rebecca thought, but because he had to coalesce his thoughts about the Aborigines, about their practices and beliefs, and he wasn't sure how it would all come out.

"What I mean is that I like Muri and his clan. In many ways they're very real, more real perhaps than we are. There's something exciting about living in nature, about walkabout. You're on your own, Rebecca, using only the skills God gave you. Me and my friends dream of being able to fend for ourselves, to hunt, to be like those heroes Hollywood is always throwing at us. But in the Back of Beyond everyone is like that. Everyone is independent. They would laugh at our heroes."

"So why do you feel so uncomfortable talking about this?" Rebecca asked, suddenly feeling sorry for her little brother. "If it's such a great life, why aren't you aching to get back there, to join Muri and his friends?"

"That's the 'sort of'," Danny admitted, standing up from

his desk and beginning to pace. When he stopped, he was standing right in front of his sister. "Rebecca, after I realized Muri and his relatives would take care of me and there was nothing to be afraid of, after that, I was still afraid."

"Why?" Rebecca prodded.

"Because their lives are based around the one thing we aren't even supposed to really think about: idol worship! If you want to be like them, then you have to be part of their spirits and their demons and their totems and their idols," he blurted out, almost in tears. "If you want to be part of them you have to throw away the Torah."

It was Rebecca's turn to feel uncomfortable. She hadn't known the depth of his feelings and how his experiences had traumatized him.

"But you didn't *do* anything, Danny," she said soothingly. "You don't have anything to feel bad about."

"You're right," he answered, calming down. "But Rebecca, I thought about it. I thought of how wonderful all those stories about demons and gods were, and I really enjoyed listening to them. I wanted to be one of Muri's tribe. That's what bothers me."

"But everyone likes stories," Rebecca tried to explain. "Everyone likes tales of gods and demons and all that stuff. But we all know it's just that — stuff. Listening to it doesn't make it true, and listening to it doesn't mean you believe it.

"Now let's stop talking about all this," she said, putting her hand on his shoulder. "You're just getting upset, and this is the most important day of your life so far."

Rebecca felt a new warmth toward her brother. She realized that he was looking for her approval, for her to say that what he felt was good and normal.

"I'm proud of you, Danny," she said in her most serious tone, "for the way you seem to have faced whatever conflicts you had and come out ahead. That's probably the best sign of maturity so far."

"So why don't I feel so mature?" he mumbled, sitting back down at his desk.

"Probably because you realize you'll never get to my level of maturity," she teased.

Danny looked up at her, opened his mouth to say something in return and then decided against it.

Maturity is also knowing when to be quiet, he thought to himself as she left his room.

EPILOGUE

Two hours later, Danny stood on the raised platform called the *bimah* at the center of his synagogue. His father and teacher were standing on either side of the bimah. In a clear, confident voice, he began to read the Hebrew words of his Torah portion, Tzav.

When he came to verse 27 — "Whosoever it be that eats any blood, that soul shall be cut off from his people" — he stopped for a moment. His teacher thought he was having trouble and prompted him with the next word. But Danny knew the words, and, more importantly, he knew the meaning of the words he was reading, probably better than anyone else in the synagogue. For the first time in a long time he felt good about himself. He had been tempted and

137

had overcome his temptation, and in so doing he had learned a lot about himself and what it means to be called "a man" in Jewish law.

He would not have to prove himself a warrior like Muri, but he was a warrior nevertheless. He had fought his demons, like Muri, and shown his bravery. And his reward, like Muri's, was to be part of his people, a son of the Covenant.

As he continued reading, he felt more confident and more at ease. Finally, he was called upon to read his *Haftorah*, the portion of the Prophets that connects with the weekly Torah reading and that every Bar Mitzvah boy reads after the Torah portion is completed. In it was the prophet Jeremiah's reprimand to the Jewish people who had begun to worship idols and believe in demons and totems.

It's all part of our history, Danny thought. Jews have always been tempted by the lure of idols, and sometimes they have even given in to their temptation.

But not me, he thought, smiling.

Not me.

BACK OF BEYOND
BUSH TALK

(Glossary of Australian words)

ABORIGINE	An indigenous black inhabitant of Australia
ALCHERA	Aboriginal period of creation
ARANDA	The tribe and language of central Australia
BACK OF BEYOND	A very out-of-the-way place
BALGEI	A boy about to become a man
BALLELI	A boy who has passed three tests that are part of the Aboriginal initiation process
BOOMERANG	Missile of thin, curved wood that can be thrown so as to return to its starting point
BUSH	Woodland, dense forest; the Outback
CORROBOREE	Festive meeting or warlike dance of the Aborigines
DIDGERIDOO	Aboriginal long, tubular wooden musical instrument with resonant sound

GUNYAH	Shelter built out of branches and grass
HUMPY	Aboriginal hut or shanty
JAMUNG UNGUR	Aboriginal blood-drinking corroboree ceremony
KALIGOOROO	Bull-roarer, noisemaker
KANGAROO	Australian marsupial with great leaping power
KOALA	Cuddly bear that lives in gum trees
KOOKABURRA	A brownish bird about the size of a crow that has a call resembling loud laughter
NALJA	The spirit of an old man with white hair, whose voice comes from the hair beneath his armpits
THE WET	Rainy season in central and northern Australia
WANJI-WANJI	Ancient Aboriginal dream dance
YAGOO	Person who helps a boy become a man
YUDU	Aboriginal command to close your eyes

ALSO
AVAILABLE
FROM

"Turn the page to Jewish pride"

THE GANG OF FOUR
Nest of the Jerusalem Eagle

by Yaacov Peterseil

Virtual Gooblyglop

by Amy Klein

Angelicum

by Lynn Sharon